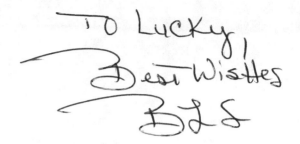
To Lucky,
Best Wishes
BLS

COLD JENA GRAY

Betty Swem

IUNIVERSE, INC.
BLOOMINGTON

Cold Jena Gray

This is a work of fiction. All of the characters, names, incidents, organizations, and dialogue in this novel are either the products of the author's imagination or are used fictitiously.

iUniverse books may be ordered through booksellers or by contacting:

iUniverse
1663 Liberty Drive
Bloomington, IN 47403
www.iuniverse.com
1-800-Authors (1-800-288-4677)

Because of the dynamic nature of the Internet, any web addresses or links contained in this book may have changed since publication and may no longer be valid. The views expressed in this work are solely those of the author and do not necessarily reflect the views of the publisher, and the publisher hereby disclaims any responsibility for them.

Any people depicted in stock imagery provided by Thinkstock are models, and such images are being used for illustrative purposes only.

Certain stock imagery © Thinkstock.

ISBN: 978-1-4620-7127-2 (sc)
ISBN: 978-1-4620-7128-9 (hc)
ISBN: 978-1-4620-7129-6 (e)

Library of Congress Control Number: 2011961973

Printed in the United States of America

iUniverse rev. date: 12/30/2011

For my brother McKenley,
I always wanted to do something extraordinary, and I think I did …

PROLOGUE

As a child, I used to dream of being someone famous, someone so important that people would watch me constantly, focusing on every move I made, but things change when you get older. Maybe it's because people don't notice you as much or maybe you just don't notice yourself. As I was transitioning, I didn't notice the change in myself right away, but then slowly, it began to take form, and I suddenly saw myself as a creature of the night, a creature that appeared innocent and harmless at first, but as you moved closer to it, you began to notice small bits and pieces of evil and ugliness. I saw the dark side of myself in the mirror many times, but I looked away and pretended that I wasn't that person, that I wasn't that unforeseen shadow that people would love from a distance but hate up close. They'd hate me. They'd hate everything about me, but did I really care? No. I really didn't care, because deep inside of me, I knew the truth, and I had embraced it a long time ago subconsciously. Deep inside, you know the truth too.

Am I cold? Well, I'm wearing a coat, hat, scarf, and even gloves. Yet, I feel cold and empty. There's a chill running through my bones that is constant, a chill that makes me want to feel the warmth of something other than your hands, those ugly hands that touched me. I hate them! Please go away! I long for a feeling of something red and hot like blood. How it flows like a river when it streams from a lifeless body. How I love it when it drips from my eyes, down my arms to the tips of my fingers, and then to the floor with each drop magnified by my obsession with it. I imagine my face being splattered with it. Am I cold? Yes, I'm cold, but not because of my body temperature or because it's below zero outside. No! That's not the kind of coldness I feel inside. It's the kind of coldness that a person feels after all the good in her is gone—after you've taken all you could and your mind begins to project its own images of the world you built that is far from the accepted reality seen by the eyes of the righteous ones.

CHAPTER ONE

Three people are standing out in the middle of the hot, windy desert. The wind is blowing fiercely, and Jena is handcuffed to a police officer's car. Tears are streaming down her cheeks. Her clothes are torn, and she is bleeding through her pants from a gash in her left knee. Jena screams out, "Were you there?"

A young boy with dark hair and sky-blue eyes stands across from her. He gives Jena a discontented look and hangs his head in shame. He bites his lips. "Where?" he asks.

Jena struggles to get loose from the handcuffs. She screams out again, "Were you there? … When he was!" Jena starts crying.

The police officer stands with his gun pointed at Jena and then at Jake to signal that no one should move. He leaves his gun pointed at Jake and turns to him. "Did you see who did this to her, young man?" Office Reyes asks.

Jake looks away and breathes hard. Then he throws his hat to the ground in frustration. The police officer walks up to him and sticks his gun in his face. "Oh, you're a tough guy? You think throwing your hat down gonna help you?" He digs his gun into Jake's left cheek. "You look at me when I'm talking to you, boy!" Officer Reyes cocks his weapon.

Jena starts to cry and screams loudly while still struggling to get loose. She pleads with Officer Reyes. "Look at what he has done to me!"

Officer Reyes turns to look at her. His face turns beet red. He turns back to look at Jake with an angry expression on his face. Jake remains silent and steps back from the officer's gun.

Jena bursts into tears. "How could you let them do this to me, Jake?"

He doesn't answer.

"You answer me!" She yells louder.

Jake looks down and rubs his head in panic. He looks up at Jena. "Yes. Yes, I was there. I was watching. I was watching him do this to you, and I couldn't stop him."

Jena looks at Jake with a disgusted, evil look on her face. Her eyes are as red as fire, and her tears are streaming harder down her cheeks. "You bastard! I'll kill you!" Jena screams. "I'll kill you. You just wait and see! I'll make you pay!"

Officer Reyes grabs Jena by the arm. "Watch your head, lady." He helps her into the police car. He puts his gun back in his holster and points at Jake. "You meet me at the station." Officer Reyes opens the driver's side door and hops inside. He sticks his head out the window. "I have some questions for you, kid. So you get your ass down to the station now."

Jake nods his head. Officer Reyes slams the car door. He stares at Jake from the car's rearview mirror. He talks to himself in the mirror. "Don't you try any funny shit either, because I'll find you and I'll do worse than she'll do to you. So if you decide to not show up, boy, I'll surely kill ya."

Jake stands at the back of the car and watches as Officer Reyes drives away. Dust hits him in the face as the car spins out of the desert. Jena turns around and stares at Jake from the back of the police car. She doesn't take her eyes off him as the car drives quickly out of the desert. Jake just continues to watch the car disappear. He stares up at the night sky, gets into his car, and then heads to the police station. Jena is sitting silently in the back of the police car when she hears a soft voice calling her.

"Jena? Jena, wake up, honey. It's time for school."

Jena suddenly awakes from her dream. "Mom?" she says in a groggy voice. "How late am I?"

Mrs. Parker stands up. "Not that late, but late." Her mother smiles and kisses her on the forehead. Jena quickly showers and begins to get dressed for school. She stands in front of her dresser mirror and stares at her red and teary eyes. She looks deep into the mirror and slowly touches her eyes. She quickly picks up her makeup kit and begins applying small dots to hide the dark circles around her eyes. The mirror has four pictures on it and a cross necklace that dangles from the top of it. She looks at her makeup and frowns. "You look ugly," she says to herself as she removes the wet towel and throws it over the mirror. She pulls her hair back into a ponytail and slips into a light-blue shirt and a checkered skirt, grabs her books, and then quickly rushes downstairs. Stumbling down the stairs, she smells the breakfast her mom is cooking. "No time for breakfast, Mom!"

She yells out as she grabs a piece of candy from the jar near the door. "I gotta run."

Mrs. Parker quickly tries to catch up with her. "Jena!" she calls in a disappointed voice.

"Sorry, Mom, I love you, but I gotta go," Jena says as she slams the front door. The school bus pulls up, and the door swings open. Ms. Amy, the bus driver, is smiling at Jena. "I see you barely made it this morning, Jena."

Jena smiles back and walks up the bus steps. Her longtime friend Jake is waiting for her. "Hi, Jake," she says as she sits down next to him.

"Hi, BFF," Jake says sarcastically.

"Oh, Jake, you're Mr. Silly today, huh?" she says and punches him on the shoulder.

"Jena, you look like you didn't get any sleep last night." He stares into her eyes.

"I didn't," she replies. "I had another dream, and strangely, it was about you." Jena stares at Jake.

"Well, I hope it was a good one." He smiles.

"It was surely interesting," Jena replies.

Sliding closer to Jena, he asks, "So, Jena, have you made any decision about my request?"

"What request, Jake?" Jena smiles and turns away.

"Ah, the request to go with me to the dance this Saturday."

Jena laughs. "Come on, I can't go to the dance with my best friend. What would people say? They'd laugh at the both of us." Jena smiles and pinches his cheek.

He turns away, his expression serious, and then he turns back to look at Jena again. "Jena, who cares about what people will say? I want to take you." He slides closer to her and slightly nudges her. In a serious voice, he says, "I want to take you to the dance, so what's wrong with that?"

Jena flashes back to her dream when Officer Reyes had her handcuffed to the police car, and tears are streaming down her cheeks while Jake stands staring at her. The bus pulls up to the school just as the first bells rings. Jena stands up. "Jake, let's talk about this after school. I got to get to class."

He stands up. "Okay," he says. Jake watches as she walks away. Two boys, Ken and Mark, walk up behind Jena and begin making obscene gestures. "Jena, you look good today, but you'd look even better with that skirt off." They both start laughing.

She turns around with her mouth open in surprise. "Leave me alone, Ken!" she says. "I'm just trying to get to class. Can't you see that?"

Ken has a malicious grin on his face. "I know, and I'm just trying to get into your panties."

Jena looks at Ken in disbelief that he just said that. Jake walks up. "Man, you better get away from Jena, because you don't want me to kick your ass."

Ken stands, looking tough, and then walks up to get in Jake's face. "Okay, tough guy, then after school, we'll see who kicks whose ass," Ken says and walks off.

Jena watches the clock throughout the day. She is tired and bewildered by her dream.

Jake and Jena pass each other throughout the day, but they barely speak. Ken passes Jake in the hallway and points at his watch. The bell rings, and Jake walks out to the bus stop. Ken walks up to him. "Are you going to kick my ass, Jake? Because if you are, then let's go."

Jake brushes up against Ken.

Principal Ricky walks out toward the bus stop. "What's going on, boys? What's the problem with you two?"

Ken steps back from Principal Ricky and adjusts his jacket. "Nothing, sir." He holds his hands up. "No problem here."

Principal Ricky puts his hands on his hips and eyes both boys. "Good, because you know Maplesville is a small town, and we small-town folk like to keep things peaceful." Principal Ricky stares at both boys. "You two got it?" Jake walks toward the bus. Jena follows. Principal Ricky steps on the bus too. "This is why today I'm riding the school bus." Everyone stares at him. The bus driver closes the door and smiles as she stares out the bus's front window. Principal Ricky stands up in front before the bus driver pulls away. "Students, I'm riding the school bus to let you kids know I'm here to support you and that I'm not going to tolerate any violence at Maple Landing High," he says while eyeing Jake and Ken. Principal Ricky sits down. The bus driver pulls away. Jake and Jena sit next to each other on the bus.

"So?" Jake says.

"So what?" Jena replies.

"So have you decided about the dance?"

"Jake, I don't want people to laugh at us."

Jake touches Jena's hand. "You mean you don't want people to laugh at you."

They both laugh. "You're a funny guy."

Jena turns and looks out the bus window. Jake begins to fantasize about Jena—just the way Jena turns her head and the sparkle in her beautiful eyes as she smiles, the softness of her neck, and even how he would kiss her if he had the chance. He fantasizes about how he'd romance Jena. He imagines himself walking to her door; she suddenly opens it wearing only an unbuttoned shirt, her long hair swaying in the wind. He slowly caresses one of her breasts while kissing her passionately. Without words being spoken, Jena motions with her finger for Jake to follow her into the house. *Like a hypnotized maniac, he follows her into her house, leans her up against a wall, and then gently kisses her. "I want you to take me right here, Jake," he imagines Jena whispering. "I want you to take me right here, right now, Jake." He moves his hands underneath her blouse,* but suddenly he is thrown back into reality when Jena's voice echoes on the bus, calling his name.

"Jake? Jake?" she calls. "Are you all right?"

Jake looks around the bus and then back at Jena. "Yeah, man, I don't know why I went into the zone, but I'm back now."

"Good," she says. "Because for a moment there, I thought you were turning into a zombie," Jena says in a creepy voice. The bus stops, and Jena gets up. "I'll see you tomorrow, zombie."

"Yeah, sure," he replies.

Principal Ricky stands up as Jena passes him. He gives her a strange look and a creepy smile and winks at her. "You have a good night now," he says as he nods his head.

Jena has an uneasy feeling. "Thanks, Principal Ricky," Jena says as she hurries off the bus.

Mr. Parker is out in the front yard playing with the dog. Jena tries to walk quickly past her father. "Something wrong, Jena?" Mr. Parker looks back at Principal Ricky standing in the bus doorway.

"No, Dad. I just had a long day at school." Jena looks back at the bus. Principal Ricky is still standing in the bus doorway, and for moment, it seems like every male on the bus is staring at her. She runs into the house and closes the door quickly.

Mrs. Parker is in the kitchen cooking dinner. Jena tries to walk upstairs without her mother noticing her. "Jena?" Mrs. Parker calls. "Jena, honey, could you come into the kitchen?"

"Yes, Mom."

Mrs. Parker is bleeding from a small cut on her hand she'd gotten while chopping chicken. Jena walks into the kitchen and sees the blood running slowly from her mother's hand. She rushes over to her. "Mom, are you all right?"

"Yes, honey. It's just a small cut," she replies while wrapping her hand with a kitchen towel. "Jena, could you go upstairs and get me the first-aid kit?"

Jena turns and runs to the upstairs bathroom to get the first-aid kit while her mom puts pressure on her wounded hand. She runs back downstairs. "Mom, you're bleeding very badly."

"Oh, it's not that bad, hon," Mrs. Parker replies. "I've had worse."

"Just hand me a big Band-aid, and I'll be just fine." Jena gets a Band-aid out of the can and helps her mom put it on. The bleeding stops. "Now, see? I'm okay." Jena and her mom laugh.

Mr. Parker walks into the kitchen. "Well, it looks like someone cut themselves again." He puts his hand on Mrs. Parker's shoulder. "I guess I'm cooking tonight," Mr. Parker says.

"Either that, or we're not going to eat," Mrs. Parker says with a smile.

Mr. Parker kisses her hand. "You know I'll cook, honey." He gives her a hug. "Now, it might not taste like much."

"Dad, I'll cook," Jena says.

"No, honey, you go do your homework. I'll cook," Mr. Parker says. "But thanks for the offer."

Jena's mom kisses her. "Yeah, honey, thanks for offering. You go on up and start your homework, and we'll call you when dinner is ready."

"Okay, Mom."

Jena walks up the stairs and stops. She glances from the top of the stairs back down at her parents. Her dad is holding her mom in his arms and kissing her. Then he kisses her cut hand again. She listens while her parents laugh as her dad scrambles around the kitchen trying to cook dinner. Jena walks to her room and picks up a picture of her parents from her dresser mirror. It is an old picture of the two of them taken when Jena was three years old. The wind blows through her bedroom window as she walks to it so she can place her face in the blowing wind. Her window curtains are blowing from side to side as she gazes out at the night sky. The wind tosses her hair around her face. She stares across the street where the McNeils live. The house is dark, and there are no cars in the driveway. She closes her window and curtain and walks back into the room. She sits on the bed.

A car horn blows loudly outside. Jena runs to her window and stands to the side so she can peek out without being observed. A car is waiting for two kids to move out of the street. Standing in his dark driveway is Mr. McNeil, staring up at Jena's window. At first, Jena isn't sure Mr. McNeil is looking at her, but the distance can't stop Jena from noticing his cold black eyes glaring at her. Jena quickly moves away from the window.

She turns off her room light, slowly walks back to the window, and peeks out again. Mrs. McNeil's car is now in the driveway. The lights in the house are on, and McNeil is no longer standing near his car. Jena slightly opens her window, and she can hear Mrs. McNeil calling for Mr. McNeil, but she gets no answer. She looks around the house, steps back in, and closes the front door. Jena continues to peek out her window, standing out of the way so no one can see her. At the edge of the house is where she spots Mr. McNeil kneeling down, hiding from his wife and peeking around the corner of the house to see if she is coming. Jena watches him carefully, trying not to be seen. She backs away from the window and sits down on her bed again. She turns on her desk lamp and opens up her math book. The phone suddenly rings, and Jena jumps. She picks up the phone, but Mrs. Parker had already answered it. Jena listens in. It is Jake's voice.

She feels at ease.

"Hello?" Mrs. Parker says.

"Hi, Mrs. Parker, can I speak to Jena?"

Mrs. Parker calls for Jena, "Jena, telephone!"

Jena answers quickly, "Hi, Jake. What's up?"

"Not much," he says. "I just was thinking about you. I wanted to hear your beautiful voice."

"Oh." Jena blushes. She tries to act normal and break the ice. "Jake, don't you have some homework to do?"

Jake doesn't answer.

"Jake, are you there?"

In a disappointed voice, he says, "Yeah, I do, but I just wanted to talk to you for a moment. I just wanted to check on you. I thought if I talked to you before you went to bed, you'd possibly dream about me again."

"Ha, ha, Jake. Very funny." Jena tries to peek out her window again while listening to Jake talk. "Jake, I like hearing your voice, but you're really, really getting weird on me. What's getting into you? You're starting to act like my creepy neighbor," she says, trying to be funny. "Are you sniffing glue again?" Jena asks with a smirk.

"Jena," Jake calls her name.

"Yes?" she replies while still peeking out the window.

"I've known you since we were in the second grade, right?"

"Yeah."

"And ever since the second grade, I've always …" He pauses. "Well, I've always thought you were a very special person."

"Jake, I know. You're special to me too."

Stumbling on his words, Jake continues, "What I mean, Jena, is that …" Jake pauses again. "Never mind."

"Jake, what are you trying to say?"

"Jena!" Mrs. Parker yells.

"Jake, wait a minute. Mom is calling me." Jena puts the phone down.

"Five minutes to dinner, Jena!" Mrs. Parker yells.

"Jake, my mom just yelled for me. It's dinnertime." Trying to make him feel more comfortable, she adds, "And can you believe my dad cooked? So what were you going to say?"

"I just wanted to tell you I appreciate your friendship."

Jena plays with the telephone cord. "Yeah, well, me too. Jake, I have to go. Mom is only giving me a few minutes to get downstairs. If you hurry, you can eat with us."

Jake is quiet. "Ah no, I think I'll pass on dinner tonight, although your mom is a great cook."

"Remember I just said my mom didn't cook tonight; she cut her hand, so my dad cooked."

"No! I'm definitely not coming," Jake says jokingly.

Jena and Jake laugh.

"Well, I have to go, Jake. I'll talk to you at school tomorrow."

"Okay, bye, Jena."

Jena hangs up the phone and heads downstairs. To her surprise, Mr. McNeil is sitting on the couch in the living room. She hesitates but walks slowly toward the kitchen.

"Hello, Jena." Mr. McNeil stands up. "Nice to see you again."

Jena stares at him. "Hello, sir," she answers. She walks into the kitchen.

Mr. Parker begins talking to Mr. McNeil. Mr. McNeil's eyes fixate on Jena as she walks toward the kitchen. He stares at her ass. Mr. Parker glances curiously at him. "Miles!" Mr. Parker says, giving Mr. McNeil a harsh look.

Trying to play it off, Mr. McNeil pats his head, "I'm just surprised at how much Jena's grown up. She's really grown into a lovely young lady."

"Yes, she has," Mr. Parker replies. "I'm very proud of her. Miles, it was nice of you to drop by, but it's dinnertime for the family."

Mr. McNeil chuckles as he tries to peek into the kitchen through the front door on his way out. Jena stands next to Mrs. Parker trying not to look in the living room. Mr. McNeil stands outside the front door but still has his body leaned up against it.

"I'll be leaving now, but let's get together for golf or catch a game," Mr. McNeil says.

"Yeah, sure, Miles, just let me know, and I'll check with the missus to see if I can get a guy's night out."

Mr. McNeil grins and pats Mr. Parker on the shoulder. "Still the dedicated husband, huh?"

"Oh yeah." Mr. Parker smiles.

"He better be!" Mrs. Parker yells from the kitchen. "It's either that or Ms. Couch tonight."

Jena makes her plate. She quickly glances from the kitchen as her father talks to Mr. McNeil through the door. She tries not to but locks eyes with Mr. McNeil. Mr. McNeil gives her a lecherous stare. Mr. Parker closes the front door and walks into the kitchen.

"That Miles hasn't changed since high school," he says. "He's still the same old jerk he's always been."

Jena sits down at the kitchen table. Mrs. Parker struggles with one hand to put the food on the table.

"Let me get that, hon. Come on, you know you can't do that."

"Yeah, Mom, you sit down, and we'll put the rest of the food out."

The doorbell rings. Mr. Parker heads for the front door. "I'll get it, Dad," Jena says. Jena goes to open the door, and it's Mr. McNeil again. Jena is a little uneasy. "I forgot my keys. Can't get in the house without those things." Mr. McNeil walks past Jena and lightly touches her. "Just let me get them really quick," he says.

"Who is it, Jena?" Mrs. Parker asks.

"It's just me, Kitty," Mr. McNeil says. "I forgot my keys."

"Well, get them, and get out; we're trying to eat dinner here."

"Sure thing, boss."

Jena stands in the doorway waiting for Mr. McNeil to get his keys. He grabs his keys, walks out the door, turns around, and winks at her.

Mr. McNeil drops his keys on the ground intentionally to stare at Jena's legs. He tries to make conversation with her, but Mr. Parker walks up and stands next to her. He picks up the keys from the ground. He locks eyes with Mr. McNeil. "Here you go, Miles. Now good night." He slams the door in his face.

CHAPTER TWO

Jena stands still for a moment at the front door. Mr. Parker grabs her and hugs her tightly, trying to make her feel better. "What a nuisance of a neighbor, huh, Jena?" He tries to make her laugh. "I made your favorite tonight."

"What? Chicken?" Jena smiles.

"Ah, no, sweet peas!" He hugs Jena and smiles.

"Oh, Dad, that's not my favorite; that's yours." Jena doesn't eat much of her dinner. She plays with the sweet peas and lets her mashed potatoes drip from her folk.

"Jena, are you all right? You barely touched your food."

"Yes, Mom. I'm all right. I'm just tired from school today, and I still have homework to do."

"Jena, why don't you just try to eat something."

"Okay, Mom," she replies.

As Mr. and Mrs. Parker talk at the dinner table, Jena remains quiet. She picks at her food, trying not to make it too obvious to her parents that she is feeling uneasy about Mr. McNeil. She thinks back to when Jake called her. *What was he really trying to say to me?* she wondered. *Today has been a weird day. It's like I woke up in another universe.*

Jena eats a spoonful of her dinner and heads upstairs. Her parents are too preoccupied with each other to notice that she hadn't touched any of her dinner. She opens her bedroom window. A cool breeze is flowing through the room. The papers on her bed begin flapping around as if there were a small storm brewing up in her room, and then rain begins to fall. Jena sits on her bed just staring out her window. She listens to the rain as it hits the windowpane and the rooftop of her house. She tries to start her homework, but the wind starts to blow very hard. She lies on her bed and gently places her head on her pillow. Jena loves the rain, because it always makes her sleepy. She begins to drift off to sleep. When Jena wakes up, it is 5:00 in the morning and she can hear her dad getting ready for work. He is humming the tune of a favorite song of his and her mother. She gets out of bed quickly to move her school papers and books from her bed to her nightstand before her dad comes into the room to wake her. She pretends that she is sleeping when her dad opens the door to her room.

"Jena?" Mr. Parker calls.

Jena pretends to wake up. "Yeah, Dad?"

"Jena, it's almost time for school," he whispers.

"Yeah, okay," she says back.

Mr. Parker is a simple, hardworking man. He is up every morning at 4:00 and always peeks in to wake Jena for school.

"Thanks, Dad," Jena says gently. "Love you. Have a good day at work."

Mr. Parker closes Jena's door and continues to hum as he walks downstairs to the kitchen to get his lunch. He opens the refrigerator and remembers that he'd forgotten to make his lunch. "Damn, I forgot Kitty's hand," he says. "I forgot to make my lunch."

Jena can hear her dad stumbling around in the kitchen trying to make his lunch quickly. She tries to get out of bed, but she is so tired she instantly falls back to sleep. She begins to dream.

She is on an airplane, and the man sitting next to her is just staring at her. He won't speak to her. She tries to ask the man questions, but all he does is stare at her. The plane begins to wobble and spin out of control and then stabilizes. Throughout the tumble of the airplane, the man just stares at her. Jena looks around the airplane, and she realizes that there are only men on the airplane. Even the flight attendant is a man. She begins to cry, and one of the men walks up to her.

"What are you doing on this airplane, young lady?"

Jena just stares at him tearfully in her in confusion.

He asks again, "What are you doing on this plane?"

"I don't know," she answers. "I don't know how I got here. I was in my room, in my bed, and now I'm on this airplane. Can you tell me how I got here and how do I get off?"

The man doesn't say a word to Jena. He stands up and walks backward, away from her. He begins shaking his head no in fear. "No, I can't because once you're on this airplane, there is no getting off. I have been trying to get off. But once you're on this plane, you will never get off. I couldn't find a way out, and you won't either." The man continues to speak, "You'll find out why one day, and by that time, it will be too late."

Jena just stares out the window of the plane and then jumps up from her seat. The man sits back down in his seat and doesn't utter another word. He sits completely still as if nothing were going on. The plane begins to spin out of control. She panics and races to the emergency door.

She begins frantically trying to open the door by beating and shaking it. "Let me out! Let me out!" she yells. She pushes harder and harder while all the men on the plane just stare at her. No matter how hard she pushes, she can't get the door open. She turns around and leans up against the door. Sweat is pouring down her face. She takes a deep breath and then walks toward the front of the plane.

All of the men on the plane just stare at her with blank looks on their faces. A sudden calmness comes over her. The men begin growling at her and clawing the seats of the plane. Jena stands and stares at the men without blinking an eye. She walks down the plane's aisle and stares each and every one of the men straight in the eyes. Jena can hear a voice calling her. "Jena! Jena!" Jena doesn't know where the voice is coming from. She sits back down in her seat and doesn't say a single word.

"Jena!" Mrs. Parker calls as she shakes her to wake her up. "Jena, wake up! You're late for school."

"What time is it?" Jena asks.

"Honey, its six thirty, and you have to be at school at seven. You need to get up and get moving. Are you feeling all right?" Mrs. Parker feels Jena's forehead.

"Yeah, Mom." Jena gets up. "I just had this weird dream. I mean *weird*. I woke up earlier when Dad was getting ready to go to work; I must have fallen back asleep. I'm sorry."

"It's okay, hon. Just get ready, and I'll take you to school."

Jena rushes to the shower. She leans one arm against the shower wall. Water runs down her face and body. Her body is tired from the night before. *What's wrong with me?* she thought.

She flashes back to her dream when she first realized that she was on the airplane: how she felt so confused and lost and then at the end of the dream, how she felt powerful and changed. She lathers soap all over her body, rinses, and dries off with a towel. There is yelling outside. Jena glances out of her bedroom window. Mrs. McNeil is yelling and pointing as she walks behind Mr. McNeil. He is walking swiftly to his car. "You're an asshole!" she yells.

Mr. McNeil turns around. "You shut your mouth!" he yells. "You're always starting something." He gets into his car and slams the door. He sits in his car. Mrs. McNeil walks back into the house. Jena quickly closes her window curtains and starts getting dressed for school.

"Jena, honey, let's get moving!" Mrs. Parker yells. "I'll get the car running and ready to go."

"Okay, Mom." Jena finishes getting dressed and throws her books into her bag. She runs downstairs.

The doorbell rings. Mrs. Parker opens the door. Mr. McNeil is standing out front wearing a light-gray suit. "Hi, Kitty. How are you this wonderful morning?"

Mrs. Parker stands in the doorway surprised. "Good morning, Miles, and I'm fine. Something wrong?"

"Uh, I was on my way to work, and I saw your car running. Going somewhere?"

Mrs. Parker sighs. "Well, Jena is running late for school, so I'm going to take her."

"Kitty, you look like you hurt your hand last night."

"Yes, I cut it slightly while cooking dinner."

"Look, I'm on my way to work; why don't you just let me drop Jena off on my way? It'll save you some gas."

Jena walks down the stairs just as Mr. McNeil is offering to take her to school.

"Jena, is that all right with you? Miles said he doesn't mind dropping you off on his way to work."

Jena stops and doesn't say anything for second. She stares down and then straight at her mom. She tries not to let her mother know she is not okay with it. "Sure, Mom; it's all right."

"Great then, I'll just turn the car right off. Thanks, Miles."

Grinning, he says, "Kitty, we all went to school together and we're neighbors. Well, come on, Jena." Mr. McNeil waves. "Let's get going and get you to school."

Jena walks cautiously across the street to Mr. McNeil's car. Mrs. McNeil walks out, and Mr. McNeil gives her a sour look.

"Hi, Jena!" Mrs. McNeil yells and waves. She walks up to the car. "Getting a ride to school?" Mrs. McNeil glances at her husband. He doesn't look at her.

"Yes, ma'am," Jena answers. "I slept late this morning."

"Oh, honey, I remember those days when I was late for class," Mrs. McNeil begins to ramble. "Ah, those days were so long ago."

Mr. McNeil becomes impatient listening to his wife. "Okay, well, we're running late." Mr. McNeil hurries his wife up.

"Don't be a stranger, Jena." Mrs. McNeil gently touches Jena's hand. "I know being a teenager can be an awkward time, but we all get through it and then we get married. What a great combination, huh?" Mrs. McNeil steps away and stares as the car drives away.

Jena sits in the car still and silent. Mr. McNeil taps his fingers on the steering wheel. Jena tries to remain quiet to get through the ride. Mr. McNeil's eyes roam down to her legs. He continues driving down the street. "So, Jena, how are things at school?" Mr. McNeil tries to make conversation.

"Good, sir."

"You don't have to call me, sir," he answers.

Jena moves slightly closer to the passenger door. Mr. McNeil makes a turn on an unfamiliar street. "Mr. McNeil, this isn't the street that goes to my school," Jena says quietly.

He looks at Jena. "Don't worry; this is just a different route I take." He looks over at her. "When I want to avoid a lot of traffic."

Jena stares out her window. He is looking at her with dirty-old-man eyes. "Don't worry, I will be at your school in no time."

Jena can see him moving his hand closer to hers. Her eyes widen. She clears her throat. He moves his hand back. "Jena, I've known your parents for a very long time. If you ever need anyone to talk to …" A car pulls in front of Mr. McNeil almost causing an accident. "What an asshole!"

Jena swallows and puts her hand over her chest.

"Are you all right?" Mr. McNeil touches Jena's leg. She moves away quickly.

"Yes," Jena says in a panic.

Mr. McNeil pulls into the school drop-off zone. The school bell has just rung, and kids are rushing to get to class. "Here we are."

Jena quickly gets out of the car and closes the door. She walks away from the car without saying good-bye to Mr. McNeil. Mr. McNeil yells,

"Jena!" She turns around. "Have a great day!" he says. She shakes her head and pulls her bag up on her shoulder.

"Thanks. Sorry, I was being rude," she says. "I'm just in a rush. Thanks for giving me a ride."

Mr. McNeil smiles and watches as she walks away. Not looking where she is going, Jena bumps into two girls strolling to class. The three girls drop their books and begin picking them up.

"Sorry, guys," Jena says. "I wasn't looking where I was walking."

"No shit," Carol says.

"Carol, be nice; she didn't mean it. Hi, my name is Chance, and this is Carol."

"My name is Jena, the girl who can't seem to look where she's walking."

All three girls laugh.

"Are you new here, Jena?" Chance asks.

"No." Jena looks at Chance strangely. "I'm not new; I've been going to this school for the last four years."

"So have we," Carol says rudely. "Where have you've been?"

"Hiding behind a rock."

"This is a big school," Carol says. "I'm sure we've passed each other at least a hundred times and just didn't know it."

"A hundred times?" Chance says.

"At least," Carol replies.

"Yeah, this is a big school," Jena says. "Well, I gotta go, guys." Jena picks up one of her books from the ground. "I'm already late." She begins walking toward her class.

"Hey, Jena!" Chance yells. "Want to hang out after school?"

Jena stands and thinks for a second. Realizing that she doesn't have many friends, she replies, "Sure."

"We'll meet here at the hit spot," Carol jokes.

"Okay!" Jena yells.

The school bells rings, and Jena begins running to her class. She's one minute late, and Mr. McDuffery isn't too happy about that. Jena tries to close the class room door quietly. "No need to be quiet, Jena, the entire class can see that you're late," Mr. McDuffery says.

"Sorry, Mr. McDuffery."

Jena moves toward her seat. "I woke up late, and I—"

Mr. McDuffery cuts her off. "Okay, Jena, thanks, but for now, just have a seat."

Jena sits next to Jake, who's grinning because she's late. There's a white rose on her desk. Jena looks at Jake and starts smiling. "Thanks, for the flower."

Mr. McDuffery catches Jena talking to Jake. "Jena, so you want to be late and talk in my class during no-talking time?" Mr. McDuffery asks. "Please be quiet. Everyone please turn to page fifty-five, chapter ten; this is where we will start today—or should have started two minutes ago." Mr. McDuffery just looks at Jena with a disapproving look on his face. Everyone in the class turns to page 55, except Jake.

Jake raises his hand.

"Yes, Mr. Paterson?"

"I apologize, Mr. McDuffery. I accidently left my book at home," Jake says.

"Accidently?" Mr. McDuffery replies.

"Yes," Jake says. "What if I accidently give you a failing grade for today?"

The class laughs.

"Just look on with Jena, please," Mr. McDuffery replies.

Jake moves his desk closer to Jena's and smiles. The class seems to last forever. Jake flirts with Jena with his eyes throughout the class. The bell rings, and everyone can't wait to get out of Mr. McDuffery's classroom. "Jena!" Mr. McDuffery calls before Jena leaves his room. "I didn't mean to embarrass you today. We all have our bad days, and yours happened to be today." Mr. McDuffery hands Jena a paper he had graded with an "A." "Maybe this will cheer you up," he says.

"Thanks, Mr. McDuffery." Jena smiles and continues walking out of the room with Jake.

"What did he say to you?" Jake asks.

"He just wanted to apologize," Jena replies.

"At least he didn't give you a late slip to take to the office like I got. "When I was late, he gave me detention," Jake says.

"Jake, you came to class when it was almost over," Jena says. "I, on the other hand, was only one minute late. I don't think you can compare the two."

They both laugh and walk toward their next class. Jena stops laughing and gets a serious look on her face "Jake, do you dream? I mean, do you have, like, weird dreams? Dreams you don't understand?"

"Sometimes, Jena."

Jena looks away, trying not to remember the horrible dream she had. Jake can see that the dream she had worries her. He tries to change the subject. "So, what are you doing after school?"

"I've been invited out," she replies.

Shocked, he asks, "By who?"

"By two girls I accidently bumped into before class. Well, let's get to class before I'm late for this one too." Jena rushes off. "See you after school, Jake."

Jake waves good-bye. Jena walks into the classroom and for the first time notices Chance sitting in the far back of the room. She walks to the back. "Hi, Chance. I never noticed that you were in this class," Jena says.

Chance stands up. "I never noticed you either."

The two girls stand there with nothing else to say. "I'm just going to take my seat." Jena points in the direction of her usual seat.

"Okay." Chance sits back down.

The school day seems to drag on, and Jena can't seem to get the dream she had out of her mind. After school, Jake is standing by the bus stop waiting for her. Jena walks up to him. "I'm so happy this day is over," she says. "Where's the bus?"

"Late, as usual," Jake says.

Principal Ricky walks out and starts yelling at some kids for fooling around.

"Jena, are you all right?" Jake asks.

"Did I tell you that I got a ride with Mr. McNeil this morning?"

"No," Jake replies.

"That guy is weird."

Jena starts telling Jake about her experience with Mr. McNeil on her way to school. Her voice fades out as he just focuses on her lips and eyes. "So that's what happened," Jena says.

Trying to act like he had been listening, he says, "Yeah, you're right; he's a real weirdo."

CHAPTER THREE

The school bus pulls up, and Jena and Jake get on the bus. Ken makes a joke from the back of the bus. "Jena, why don't you come back here and sit with us?"

"No, thanks, Ken." Everyone on the bus starts laughing.

Jake turns around. "Man, just leave her alone."

Ken backs down. "Oh, Jake, come on, we're just joking around."

Jake looks around the bus. "Who are *we*? Because you're the only one talking." Jake turns back around. "Okay, man. I'll leave your girlfriend alone."

Jake stands up.

"Jake, stop." Jena touches his arm.

The bus driver yells out to Jake to take his seat and for Ken to shut his mouth. Jake sits down, and Jena sits next to him. "Hey, do you think it was Ken who gave me the flower?" she whispers.

"Maybe it was Principal Ricky," Jake says in a joking tone.

"What?" Jena replies. "What would make you think it was Principal Ricky?" Jena asks.

Jake shrugs his shoulders. "It was what he said to you before we got on the bus. Do you remember?" Jake replies. "And the fact that he's creepy. Just look at him."

"Just think of what you're saying, Jake? You think that Principal Ricky has a crush on me?"

"Yeah," Jake replies. "A big huge one." Jake starts laughing.

"Stop laughing, Jake." Jena tugs on his shirt.

"So it could be him or not, but if it is him, I'll take care it, Jena, if you want me to."

"What are you gonna do?"

"Well, I can walk up to Principal Ricky and say, 'Hey, leave Jena alone; she's my girl.'"

Jena starts laughing. "Jake, Principal Ricky knows we aren't dating; he was our second-, third-, and fourth-grade teacher, and now he's our principal. He knows we're just good friends."

"Yeah, but … maybe that will make him back off."

"Just don't do anything, Jake," Jena says. "Because I still don't know for sure if it was Principal Ricky who sent me the flower, and I don't want to get you in trouble. Besides, look at this flower. They both look at the flower on her lap. "It's beautiful, and I'm just glad someone out there is thinking of me." She looks up at him with a smile.

Time suddenly freezes for Jake for a moment; he is mesmerized by her smile. He examines every curve of her mouth, every dimple on her face, and those eyes, those beautiful eyes just keep him hypnotized. Jena snaps her fingers. Jake bounces back to reality. "Even if it's Principal Ricky who sent them, so what? I have a secret admirer who finds me attractive." Jena grabs Jake by the nose and squeezes.

Jake just looks at Jena and nods his head. He thinks to himself, *I love you, Jena. If only I could tell you that I sent the rose and if only I could tell you how much I want you and how much I love you.*

The bus stops. Jena stares at her house. "Okay, here's my stop." She stands up. "See you tomorrow, stud. I gotta go in to do some serious homework. Oh wait!" Jena stops.

"What?" Jake asks.

"I was supposed to be hanging out with those two girls I met, Chance and Carol. I forgot about it because of the whole flower thing. Oh well." Jena walks off the bus. "I'll see tomorrow. Bye, Jake."

Jena gets off the bus and walks toward her house. Mr. McNeil is standing in his front yard. He has a dozen roses in his hand. The bus driver pulls away, and Mr. McNeil waves and walks toward Jena. Jena tries to hurry inside. "Hey, Jena!" Mr. McNeil calls. He runs to catch up with her.

"Hi," she answers, out of breath.

"Wow, I haven't seen you since when?" he says, trying to make a joke. "Oh, I know, since I dropped you off this morning." Mr. McNeil stands and speaks to Jena while tightly gripping the dozen roses in one hand. He holds his briefcase in the other. Jena stares at the roses, which look similar to the rose she has.

"Nice flowers, Mr. McNeil," she says in a hesitant voice.

"These are for my wife."

Jena sighs with relief.

"I thought I'd make up for our fight this morning."

Jena stares intently at the roses Mr. McNeil is holding. The roses seem similar to the rose left on her desk, and it looks like one of the roses is missing from the bunch. "Mr. McNeil, it looks like the flower shop may have shorted you one rose."

Mr. McNeil looks at the rose bunch. "Oh, damn, you're right, Jena. I paid for a dozen, and I got eleven." He widens his eyes at her. "Well, hopefully the little missus won't look as hard as you did and notice the missing rose." Mr. McNeil's eyes zoom in on Jena's rose. "Looks like someone was thinking of you today too, huh?" Mr. McNeil points a finger at Jena's flower.

"Yes, someone left me a rose on my desk. I don't know who it was, but I'm sure whoever it was, was only trying to be nice."

Mrs. McNeil pulls up in her car. Mr. McNeil tries to hide the flowers behind his back. Mrs. McNeil gets out of the car, and Mr. McNeil walks over to her and hands her the roses. They begin kissing and walking away toward the house. They pay no attention to Jena. She just watches the two laugh and cuddle as they walk into the house.

Jena thinks to herself, *There is no way it could be Mr. McNeil. Wow, just this morning, she was a raging bull and he was the biggest jerk, but look how in love they seem to be!* Jena walks away shaking her head. "It wasn't him. Why would Mr. McNeil want to give me a flower?"

The mystery of the flower stays on Jena's mind. As she starts to walk toward the house, a car pulls up and starts honking its horn very loudly. A voice yells out to Jena, "Hey, Jena! You stood us up!" It was Chance and Carol.

Very surprised, Jena says, "Hey, guys, how did you know where I live?"

"Jena, this is a small town. Everyone knows where everyone lives," Chance replies. "So are we still on?"

"Yeah, sure. Just let me put my stuff in the house and tell my mom I'll be back later." Jena walks into the house. She can smell the aromas of her Mom's great cooking coming from the kitchen. "Mom! Mom!" Jena yells.

"I'm upstairs," Mrs. Parker yells back.

Jena quickly runs upstairs. "Mom, can I go out for a little while? I met these two girls at school, and well, you know, I don't usually go anywhere, so I told them I would hang out today."

"Sure, Jena, it's okay with me," she replies. "I'm sure your dad will be fine with it too, so go have some fun for a change. Just make sure you're home by dinner."

Jena runs up to her room quickly to put her stuff away. She glances into the mirror, brushes her hair, pats on a little makeup, and then runs back downstairs. "See ya, Mom!" she yells.

Jena hops into the backseat. Chance turns the music way up, and the two girls in front start singing along with the song. Chance yells to Jena over the music, "Jena, do you like this song? This song really rocks."

Jena just nods her head.

Chance tries to speak over the music. So you like pool?"

"What?" Jena replies.

Chance turns the radio down. "Do you like playing pool?"

"Oh yeah, it's cool," Jena replies.

"Jena, I'm so glad you could hang out with us," Chance says.

"So where are we going?" Jena asks.

"We're going to a place called Topaz. It's like a bar, but kids our age can hang out there. Do you know how to shoot pool?"

"I've never played pool before," Jena replies.

"We'll teach you. Right, Carol?" Chance looks over to Carol.

Carol looks back at Chance with a smirk. "You mean Ken will teach her; he's the expert."

Jena leans forward. "Why is Ken going to be there?"

Chance and Carol ignore her. "Hey, Chance, maybe we'll see that hot guy again too."

The two girls start laughing. "Maybe he can teach all of us a thing or two."

"You're bad, Carol," Chance says.

The two girls start laughing louder. Jena just sits quietly for a moment and then laughs lightly, pretending to get the joke. Chance pulls up to Topaz; it is a biker club located across town. Several older male and female bikers are standing around their bikes drinking and smoking cigarettes.

Jena has a frightened look on her face. "Guys, is this place safe?" Jena asks.

"Is anywhere safe?" Carol replies. "Yes, it's safe, Jena," she continues. "We come here to hang out all the time." Carol looks back at Jena with a disappointed look on her face. "Are you scared?"

"No," Jena replies.

"Do you think we would bring you to an unsafe place?" Carol is trying to intimidate Jena. Jena just stares at her.

"I don't see any other kids our age here." Jena looks at the older bikers.

Carol tries to get confrontational. "Maybe there are inside, Jena."

"Carol, please just shut up." Chance points a finger at her.

A crowd of high school guys walks out of the building. "See, look, there's Ken and his friends."

Oh great, Jena thinks.

"What's wrong, Jena?" Chance asks.

"Oh, Ken is just the only person in the world who doesn't like me. He picks on me almost every day," Jena replies.

"Not today, Jena." Chance grabs Jena and pulls her closer to her. "Because you're my friend now and you're with us. Besides, Ken's my boyfriend, and I'll kick his butt if he does or says anything bad to you."

Jena is surprised. She thinks to herself, *I never saw Ken with Chance, but I guess I never really paid attention either, because I never noticed Carol and Chance at school. How is that possible? I mean, where have I been for the last four years?*

Ken walks up to the car and kisses Chance on the lips. "Hi, babe."

Carol tries to make him take notice of her. "What about me, Ken?"

In a low voice, he says, "Hi, Carol," while still kissing Chance. He's trying to ignore her. He glances in the backseat and notices Jena. "What is she doing here?" Ken asks.

"We asked her to hang out with us," Carol replies quickly.

Chance grabs his face. "And you better not say one damn thing to her or I'll kick your ass."

"Calm down, Chance," Carol replies. "He's not going to do anything."

Chance kisses Ken on the cheek. "Ken, she's our friend, so that means you be a nice little boyfriend, or I may become an enraged girlfriend, and you don't want that." Chance grabs Ken's jaw and shakes his head. Then she kisses his lips really hard.

"Of course not, babe. You know I don't want my lady being mad at me." Ken gives his buddy standing next to him a thumbs-up. "I'll be nice tonight."

"No, Ken, you will be nice always. Got it?" Chance says.

Ken kisses Chance on the forehead. "Got it," he says. Trying to be friendly, he says, "So what's up, Jena?" He reaches his hand out to her.

She lightly touches him.

"Don't worry, I promise I will be a complete gentleman."

Ken's other friends yell out to him. "Hey, man, let's go inside!"

"Hold on, guys!" He yells back. "Let's go, babe."

Carol quickly gets out of the car, and Ken just stares at her. He opens the door for Chance. "You too, Jena. Let's roll." Ken keeps the car door open for Jena. He puts his arms around Chance and whispers something into her ear. Chance smiles and kisses him again. Carol becomes angry. Inside the building, country music is playing, and two drunken bikers are trying to dance without falling down.

"Look at those two freaks!" Ken says. He starts laughing out loud.

"Is there something funny, kid?" one of the drunken men asks.

"No," Chance says quickly to avoid a confrontation.

"Well, yeah," Ken says.

"Ken, stop!" Chance yells. She doesn't want him to start a fight.

He continues, "We're laughing at your stupid asses trying to dance," Ken says to the man.

One of the drunken men walks toward Ken. The club bouncer begins to move closer to him, ready to intervene. "Hey, Ernie, just cool it man, because you know I'll put your ass out," the bouncer says, holding a pool stick. "And, kid?" The bouncer points at Ken. "Shut up because I'll put your ass out too. You're lucky I let you stay. If I didn't know your bro Ted, you and your monkey friends would be out of here. So don't say another damn word, all right?"

"Got it."

The bouncer walks away and knocks one of the drunken bikers down. "Get up, you jerk."

Ken wraps his arms tightly around Chance and tries not to say anything. The two drunken bikers continue to dance. Ken reaches for the pool stick. "See, I told you that those two bikers were freaks," Ken says.

"Well, if they're freaks, and they're in this bar, then what are we?" Carol asks.

"We are a group of high school seniors that makes this place feel like gold," Ken replies.

All of them except Jena start high-fiving and laughing.

"Now, let's shoot some pool," Carol says.

Ken pays for the pool table and grabs the pool sticks.

"Okay, who's going to teach Jena how to play pool?" Chance asks. Everyone stares at one another. Chance and Carol stare at Ken.

"Come on, guys." Ken raises both his hands up to gesture that he doesn't want to teach Jena.

"It's okay, guys; I really don't want to play," Jena says. Chance gives Ken a dirty look.

"You're playing pool, young lady. Come here, Jena." Ken reaches for her. "You get in front, and I'll stand behind you and show you how to play pool."

"Don't get too happy, Ken." Chance folds her arms. Ken blows her a kiss and smiles. He stands behind Jena with his body close enough to embrace hers. Jena feels a little uncomfortable, but she continues to allow Ken to teach her. Ken puts his hand on Jena's and shows her how to shoot a ball into the pool table pocket. Just then, Jake walks in and is instantly angry that Ken is embracing Jena. Jake goes crazy with the thought of Ken touching Jena. In his mind, Ken is pretending to teach her how to play pool only to get close to her. Jake stares angrily at the both of them, and he walks up to the pool table. Jena looks up at Jake in surprise. Ken backs away from Jena.

"Jake, what are you doing here?" Jena asks in a surprised voice.

"Jena, the question isn't what am I doing here, but what the hell is this jerk doing touching you?" Unable to hold back his anger, Jake yanks the pool stick out of Jena's hand. Ken pushes Jena out of the way and picks up a pool stick. The two boys stand face-to-face, ready to fight.

CHAPTER FOUR

Jena tries to get in between Ken and Jake. "Jake, I came out here with Chance and Carol. I didn't know Ken was Chance's boyfriend."

Jake looks over to Chance.

"What are you doing here? How did you know I was here?" Jena asks.

"I went by your house, and your mom told me you had left with two girls. I figured it was Chance and Carol, and since I knew where they hang out, I decided to come by to surprise you, but I guess I got the surprise with Ken's arms all wrapped around you."

"Jake, it's not like that," Jena tries to calm things down. "Ken was just showing me how to play pool."

"I bet," Jake replies.

"Man, why don't you get the heck out of here?" Ken says, as he moves closer to Jake, pushing Jena out of the way.

"You're being silly, Jake." Jena tries to intervene again.

"Am I?" Jake stares back at Ken.

"Yes, you're being silly." Jena grabs the pool stick out of his hand. "Jake, let's just leave, okay?"

Jena tries to grab Jake's arm, but he pulls it away.

"Ken walks over to Jake. "What's your problem, man? I mean, do you really want to start some shit in this place?" Ken gets closer to Jake's face.

"Do you?" Jake replies,

"Look, I was just showing her how to play a simple game of pool, and here you come, trying to play the hero, as if you were rescuing someone."

"Ken, stop! We don't want a fight!" Chance breaks in.

Ken turns and looks at Chance with an angry face. "Look, Chance, he's the one who came here and interrupted our pool game, and you want me to stop?"

In a panicked voice, she says, "Yes, I do."

Ken pokes Jake in the chest. "Well, I'm not going to. I gonna shut this guy up once and for all," Ken replies.

"Jena, get out of the way before you get hurt!" Carol yells.

Chance grabs Jena and pushes her out of the way. "Guys, stop!" Jena yells, trying to keep the two boys from getting any closer. "Jake, let's just go; let's just leave this place and go home," Jena says, her voice shaking with fear. "You don't have to fight."

The bouncer comes out from his boss's office in the back of the club. "Hey, you two!" he yells. "You fight in this bar, and I'll kick both of your asses."

Neither Jake nor Ken back down. The bouncer walks over. "You think I'm kidding? I will mess the both of you up!" He's getting angry. "You know what? All of you get the hell out of here!" A sudden noise of glass breaking comes from the other side of the room. Two bikers are about to fight. One of the bikers punches another one in the stomach and then the face, picks him up, and throws him over the bar. The bouncer runs over to try to stop the two bikers from fighting. Chance grabs Ken's hand to pull him away, but he jerks away from her. Jena is still in the middle of the two, and she puts her hands on Ken's and Jake's chests to try to stop them from getting any closer, but Ken pushes her out of the way and she falls to the floor. Jake throws a punch and hits Ken in face, and the two boys start fighting. Ken picks up a chair and hits Jake over the back. Jake falls to the floor, and Ken begins punching him in the face and stomach. Chance runs over and tries to stop Ken, but Ken's friends pull her back.

"Let them fight," one of the guys says.

The bouncer is still trying to stop the two bikers from fighting. He begins fighting with the both of them. Chairs and glasses are broken everywhere. One of the bikers pulls out a knife. He stabs the other biker in the stomach and cuts the bouncer on the arm. The bouncer stares down at his bleeding arm. He walks up to the biker, grabs his neck, and chokes him up against a wall. The biker stabs the bouncer in the shoulder. The knife sticks there, and the bouncer continues to choke the biker, who's still pressed against the wall. The bouncer lifts the biker up in the air by the neck and throws him over the bar. The biker slams into the liquor bottles behind the bar before hitting the floor. The stabbed biker lies bleeding on the floor. Ken is still beating on Jake. Jake is unable to move. His face is bruised, and his nose is broken. Jena, Chance, and Carol are all screaming for Ken to stop, but Ken's friends hold the girls back. The bouncer turns around; he still has the knife in his shoulder. He runs over to Ken, picks him up by his jacket, and throws him over a table. Ken hits his head and is knocked unconscious. Jake is on the floor still in pain from all the hits he took from Ken. Chance runs over to Ken. Carol calls 911 for an ambulance.

Jena kneels down to help Jake, and she starts crying. "Jake, oh my God! Jake, please be all right! I'm so sorry, Jake."

Chance tries to talk to Ken, but he does not answer her. Tears are flowing down Jena's face. "Jake, please say something, please," she pleads.

Jake tries to open one of his eyes. The police and paramedics come rushing into the room. One of the EMS teams checks Ken, and the other checks Jake's vitals. Ken is still unconscious. The EMS team quickly puts Ken on a stretcher to take him to the hospital. Jake is put on another stretcher. Both of the boys are hauled in the same ambulance to the hospital. EMS then checks the stabbed biker on the floor. The biker is pronounced dead at the scene. Another team is called in to treat the bouncer for the stab wound and the other biker, who is knocked out behind the bar.

A police officer interviews Chance, Carol, Jena, and the bouncer to find out what happened. It is Officer Reyes, but Jena doesn't recognize him from her dream. He walks over to the bouncer who is being treated by one of the paramedics. "So what happened here, Ernie?" Officer Reyes asks.

The bouncer looks around the room with the knife still lodged in his arm. "Well, it looks like we had a fight. Isn't that obvious, Reyes?"

"Look, just because you've been stabbed doesn't mean I won't haul your ass downtown," Officer Reyes replies. "So while we are waiting for an ambulance to come get your sorry ass, how about telling me what the hell happened here?"

Ernie sighs. "We had several fights, and as you can see, I got stabbed trying to break up the fights." He continues, "That's all I'm going to say. If you want more, you'll have to talk to my lawyer."

Officer Reyes looks around the room. He stands quietly staring at the bouncer. "I'll see you again." He calls for the ambulance to come get the bouncer and take him to the hospital. Officer Reyes walks over to Jena, who is still in shock. "Hello, my name is Officer Reyes," he says.

Jena doesn't say anything. "What's your name, ma'am?"

Jena has tears in her eyes. "My name is Jena."

"Jena what?" Officer Reyes asks.

"Jena Parker."

"Okay, Jena Parker, can you tell me what happened here?"

Jena tries to talk though her sobs, but she can't get the words to come out. "Ah … Well …" She struggles to speak.

Officer Reyes stands and stares at Jena with a pen and pad in his hand.

"Ken and Jake were arguing over me, and then they got into a fight. Ken hit Jake with a chair. Jake fell to floor and …" Jena begins crying harder. "And I don't know … I don't know."

Trying to comfort Jena, he says, "Okay, Jena, just take your time; everything will be all right." Officer Reyes pats Jena on the shoulder.

Chance and Carol walk over to Jena and Officer Reyes. "Were you two young ladies here when the fights broke out?" Officer Reyes asks.

Chance and Carol look at one another. Before Chance can answer, Carols says, "Yes, but we didn't see everything that was going on. I mean, we just don't know who started the fight," she adds.

Jena just stares at both Chance and Carol in disbelief. "Okay, so what did you see?" Officer Reyes asks.

"Well, Officer, there was so much going on at the same time that we just don't know what happened," Chance repeats.

"Yes, Officer, there was just too much going on, and, well, we couldn't keep track of everything," Carol says.

Officer Reyes taps his pen on his head. Chance stares at Carol and Jena. Jena looks at Officer Reyes with tears in her eyes. She shifts her gaze to Chance and Carol. "Can we leave?" Chance asks. "One of the guys who got hurt is my boyfriend, and I'm very worried about him," Chance pleads.

"I will need both of your full names and parents' phone numbers," Officer Reyes says.

"I'm Carol Jones."

"I'm Chance Middleton."

"And what are the names of the boys who were fighting?" Officer Reyes asks.

"Ken Marks and Jake Paterson," Chance replies. "Now can we leave?"

"Okay, you girls can go, but you are directed to go straight home to your parents first," Officer Reyes replies. He walks away to speak to the other officers on the scene.

"Let's go, guys. We need to get to the hospital."

"Didn't you hear what that police officer just said? We have to go home first," Jena says, still sobbing.

"He said we should go home to our parents, not that we had too. He's not my dad," Carol says.

"He's going to tell our parents," Jena replies.

"So what? I need to see Ken, and you need to see Jake," Chance replies.

"So? He's gonna tell our parents anyway," Carol says.

"Let's just go to the hospital for a second, and then we'll go home," Chance insists.

"No," Jena says in an angry voice. "You guys take me home first. I'm not gonna get myself into any more trouble."

"Okay, we will drop you off, and then we'll go," Chance says.

The three girls walk out of the building. It is getting dark outside, and the parking lot is empty except for their own car, the police cruisers, and the owner's car. Jena quickly jumps into the car's backseat. Sitting quietly in the backseat of the car, Jena is upset about Jake getting hurt. She thinks back to the funny conversation they'd had on the bus earlier about the mysterious flower and how close Jake and she had become over the years. She can see Chance looking back at her in the rearview mirror. She becomes angry thinking about when Officer Reyes asked Chance and Carol what happened in the club and they both lied and how she felt pressured not to tell Officer Reyes that Chance and Carol were liars, that they saw everything and they knew what really happened. Chance pulls over to the curb in front of Jena's house. Jena gets out and begins to walk away.

"Jena, I'm sorry."

Jena turns around. Tears flow down her cheeks. She doesn't say anything. Chance drives away. Mr. McNeil is standing in his front yard watering his plants. He stares at the two girls as they drive away. Jena walks into her house, closes the door, and then turns around to look through the door peephole. Mr. McNeil is standing in his front yard staring over at Jena's house. He grips the water hose tightly as the water runs down his pants to his shoes. Jena breathes quickly and panics. She looks down to the floor and turns around to lean against the door.

CHAPTER FIVE

Jena can feel her heart beating out of control. She takes in a deep breath and then turns around to peek through the hole again.

"Jena, what are you doing?" Mrs. Parker asks. She's standing in the kitchen doorway waiting for her. Jena turns around quickly. Mrs. Parker walks toward Jena. She can tell Jena is scared.

"Jena, are you all right?" Mrs. Parker touches her forehead. "We got a call from an Officer Reyes that some high school kids were involved in a fight at a bar. What's going on?"

Jena just breaks down in tears. Mrs. Parker puts her arms around her and walks her to the living room couch. Mrs. Parker sits Jena down on the couch and takes a seat next to her. "Jena, what happened, honey? The officer said Jake, Ken, and some other people at the bar got hurt, that they're both on their way to the hospital."

"Yes, Mom, they're both hurt, and it's all because of me! It's all my fault!" Jena cries.

"What do you mean it's your fault?" Mrs. Parker asks. "How do you have anything to do with these two boys being in the hospital?"

"Because they were fighting over me, Mom!" Jena yells. "I went to this place with Chance and Carol, and Ken was there. Mom, I didn't know Ken was going to be there, but then Jake showed up and he saw Ken helping me learn how to play pool, and I guess he got mad and jealous. They got into an argument, and then it led to a fight. Oh, Mom, it was just so terrible, Jake getting hurt." Jena wipes the tears from her eyes and cheeks.

Mrs. Parker pats Jena on the back. "Oh, Jena, it's not your fault. You didn't make those two boys fight. They decided to fight on their own. You can't take responsibility for someone getting hurt if you didn't cause it. I'm sorry Jake and the other kid got hurt, but both of them made a choice to fight." Mrs. Parker stands up. "I'm sure Jake will be all right."

Jena stands up too. "Mom, I need to go see Jake. Officer Reyes told all of us to go home first, but I really need to know Jake is all right."

"Jena …" Mrs. Parker answers in concerned voice.

"Mom, I *have* to go see him. Please take me," Jena pleads.

"Jena, I think I should speak to your father about what happened today first."

"Mom, please! If you tell Dad now, I'll never see Jake. Please, Mom, just take me up there. Can't we just tell Dad later?" Jena runs and hugs her mom tightly.

"Okay, Jena, I'll take you to see Jake. First, let me call Mrs. Paterson to let her know we are going to the hospital to see Jake."

"Mom, Mrs. Paterson is probably at the hospital with Jake."

"Yes, you're right. Well, let's go." Mrs. Parker grabs her purse and her keys, and they both head outside to get into the car.

Mr. McNeil is still standing in his yard. Jena gets into the car. Just as Mrs. Parker opens her car door, Mr. McNeil calls to her, "Hey, Kitty! Is there something going on, something wrong with Jena?"

Trying to avoid him, she says, "No, we're just headed out. Be back later." Mrs. Parker quickly gets into her car to head to the hospital.

The hospital emergency parking lot is crowded. Mrs. Parker turns in. "Oh, Jena, this doesn't look like a good night for the hospital." They walk into the hospital building. Several friends of Ken's and Jake's are standing outside. Jena holds her head down as she walks into the hospital building.

"Jena!" Chance calls. "What's up?"

"I'm here to see Jake," Jena answers softly.

"I went to see Ken, but his mother wouldn't let me see how he was doing." Chance grabs Jena's hand. "I don't think she likes me very much."

Jena puts her hand on Chance's shoulder. "If I see or hear anything, I'll let you know."

"Thanks, Jena," Chance replies.

Jena and Mrs. Parker walk to the hospital emergency room counter. The nurse is sitting at the desk reading a magazine. Mrs. Parker taps on the counter.

"Yes, may I help you?" the nurse asks.

"Yes, we are friends of Jake Paterson. Could you tell us what room he is in?"

The nurse types in Jake's name. "He is on the second floor, room 201."

"Thank you." Mrs. Parker reaches for Jena's hand. "Come on, Jena, let's go upstairs."

Mrs. Parker and Jena walk to the elevator and get in. Jena notices that a man has followed them onto the elevator. The elevator doors close. The man stands next to the wall and stares at Jena. Trying not to look at the man, Jena pushes the second floor button and then turns to the man. "I'm going to the second floor as well," the man whispers to Jena. The elevator door opens at the second floor, and Jena and Mrs. Parker walk off the elevator. Jena looks back, but the man isn't there.

"Mom, what happened to the man that was on the elevator?" she asks.

"What man, Jena?" Mrs. Parker replies as she looks back. "It was only you and I on that elevator." She gently grabs Jena's face. "Are you all right, honey? Are you up to this? Maybe we should go home. You've had a very stressful day. Why don't you just lie down and see Jake tomorrow."

"Mom, we're already here, and I have to see Jake tonight," Jena insists. "I'm sure he is waiting for me to come see him. If I was hurt in the hospital, I know he would do whatever it took to see me."

Feeling sympathy for Jena's pain, she says, "I understand, honey. I know you care about Jake."

"I'm all right, Mom. I mean, I was upset earlier, and I still am a little, but Jake and I are friends and I need to be here for him now," Jena replies.

Jena and Mrs. Parker walk down the hall toward Jake's room. Jake's father is standing in the hallway speaking to his doctor. Mr. Paterson stops what he's doing to speak to Mrs. Parker and Jena as they walk toward him. Mr. Paterson walks up and gives Jena a hug.

"Jena, are you all right?" Mr. Paterson asks.

"Mr. Paterson, I'm so sorry for what happened to Jake," Jena replies.

"It's okay, Jena. Jake is barely speaking, but he told us it was his fault and not yours." Mr. Paterson hugs Jena again.

Mrs. Paterson walks out of Jake's hospital room. She hugs Jena too. "Jena, are you all right, honey? Hi, Kitty," she says as she hugs Mrs. Parker.

Mrs. Parker reaches for Cindy Paterson's hand. "Jena and I wanted to come and see how Jake was doing. Jena is very worried about him."

"Well, Jake's doing okay," Cindy replies. "As well as can be expected."

Jena walks closer to Jake's room door. Jake is hooked up to several tubes and machines. His eyes are closed. "Can I see him?" she asks.

"Sure," Cindy answers. "His eyes are closed, but he's kind of awake. The nurse just gave him a mild sedative to help him sleep through the pain. I'm not sure how long he will be awake."

She walks through Jake's hospital room door and up to his bedside. Jake's eyes are closed, and the television in the room is on. His face has some bandages on it, and one of his arms is in a sling. Jena gently touches his hand. Jake doesn't move. She stands over him, watching him sleep. Jake smiles, and in groggy voice, he tries to speak. "I bet you thought I was asleep," he says. "I just wanted to feel your hand on mine without saying anything, just for a moment."

"I'd squeeze it if I thought it wouldn't bring you more pain."

He barely whispers back, "Hi, you." Jake slightly and painfully smiles at Jena.

"Jake, I'm so sorry."

Jake shakes his head slowly. He whispers to her, "No, don't be." His eyes begin to close. The medicine the nurse gave him is beginning to take full effect. He falls asleep.

"Rest, my sweet Jake." Jena gently reaches over to kiss Jake on the forehead, and then she turns to walk out of the room. Jena overhears Mrs. Patterson speaking to her mother.

"Jake's doctor said that he may be in the hospital for at least a week."

Jena walks toward them. "He fell asleep on me, but I think he'll be all right," she says in a relieved voice. Mrs. Parker and the Patersons continue to talk.

Jena notices a girl from her school dressed as a candy striper. She walks over to speak to her. "Susan, is that you?" Jena asks.

"Hi, Jena," Susan replies.

"What are doing here, and why are you dressed like that?" Jena asks.

"I'm a volunteer for the hospital, Jena. You know, a candy striper." Susan turns away to show off her work outfit. "Like my outfit?"

"So you're here all the time?" Jena asks.

"No, just sometimes after school and on the weekend, if they need me."

"Can anyone be a candy striper?" Jena asks.

Susan lifts one of her eyebrows. "Yeah, I guess so. Just go see Ms. Louis," Susan says. "She's our warden."

The girls laugh.

"Well, I have to get back to work. See ya."

"Yeah, see ya." Jena waves good-bye.

Susan turns back around. "Hey, don't worry, Jena. I'm working this floor tonight. I'll keep an eye on him."

"Thanks, Susan," Jena walks back over to where her mother and the Patersons are still talking.

"Ready to go?" Mrs. Parker asks.

"Yes, I guess so, Mom."

"Don't worry, Jena; everything will be all right," Mrs. Patterson says as she and Mr. Patterson walk back into Jake's hospital room.

"Good night, guys," Mr. Paterson says.

Jena and Mrs. Parker begin walking toward the elevator. "Feel better now?" Mrs. Parker asks as she hits the button on the elevator.

"Yes, I do, Mom. Thank you for bringing me."

Jena and her mother step into the elevator. Jena looks at her mom and for the mysterious man who got on with them earlier. The man never shows up again. *I know I saw him,* Jena thinks. *Maybe I'm just stressed.* "Mom, what do you think about me becoming a candy striper?" Jena asks. Mrs. Parker just stares at her with a surprised expression on her face.

CHAPTER SIX

Mrs. Parker smiles at Jena.

"Mom, what are you smiling about? Is there something wrong with me wanting to help in the hospital?"

"No, but it does seem kind of sudden, Jena. This wouldn't have anything to do with Jake being in the hospital, would it?"

"Well, yes and no," Jena replies. The elevator door opens, and Jena and Mrs. Parker walk to the hospital parking lot. Jena continues to try to convince her mother. "I mean, I want to see Jake and I want to do something good at the same time. So what could be better than volunteering in the hospital to help sick people?" Jena says.

"You had a traumatic experience, and now you want to do something good. I think you wanting to help others can be a noble thing. My answer is yes."

Jena jumps up and down. "I still need to speak to your father about it, okay?"

"Yes," Jena confirms.

"Yes," Mrs. Parker answers again, this time with a bigger smile.

"Mom, could we stop by to see Ms. Louis about me volunteering before we leave the hospital?" Jena asks.

"Sure, honey, let's find out where her office is located." Jena and Mrs. Parker walk the hospital halls to find Ms. Louis. They stop several hospital staff members who instruct them to go to another person for the information. Jena and her mother stop by the hospital patient information desk to try to find Ms. Louis's office. A young male nurse is sitting behind the nurses' station desk, talking on the phone.

They stop to ask him for the location of Ms. Louis's office. "Sarah, if you leave the house this time, I'm not taking you back!" the man speaks angrily into the phone. "I mean it!"

Mrs. Parker stares at him. He slams the phone down. "Can I help you?" he asks in a rude voice.

Stunned, Mrs. Parker is silent for second. "We are trying to find Ms. Louis's office. Can you help us?"

"Behind you."

"What?" Mrs. Parker has a puzzled looked on her face.

The male nurse points. "Her office is right behind you."

"Thank you," Mrs. Parker says. Jena just doesn't say anything.

The male nurse slams the phone down again. He gets up and walks away from his desk. "Damn woman."

"Sam? Sam?" Ms. Louis walks out and calls for the male nurse who just keeps on walking.

"I'll be back, Ms. Louis. Just going to the bathroom!" the male nurse yells.

She turns to Jena and Mrs. Parker. "How may I help you?"

"We are looking for Ms. Louis," Mrs. Parker says.

"I'm Ms. Louis." She looks directly at Jena. "Let me guess, you want to be a candy striper."

"Yeah," Jena replies.

"Well, come in, young lady."

Jena is nervous.

"Have a seat." Mrs. Parker stands in the hallway to wait for Jena. "Well, I only have one question that I ask before my volunteers start, and it is: why do you want to be a volunteer?" Ms. Louis smiles as she leans over her desk a little.

Jena turns around to look at her mother and then back at Ms. Louis. "Well, the reason why I want to be a volunteer is because ..." Jena stops for a second. "It's because I ..." Ms. Louis stares intently at Jena. "The truth is someone I care about very much just got hurt, and it made me realize how important life is, so I want to do something to help," Jena replies.

Ms. Louis nods her head in agreement. "Jena, that was a very good response. The hospital is always looking for good people. I would be happy to have you as a volunteer," Ms. Louis says. "I just have one more question." Jena stares at her curiously. "Can you start tomorrow?"

Mrs. Parker sticks her head in the door.

"Mom, can I start tomorrow?"

"Yes. Why not? I'm sure your dad will be all right with it."

Ms. Louis walks out of her office with Jena and Mrs. Parker. Sam, the nurse, still hasn't returned to the nurses' station. "Where the heck is Sam? It was nice meeting you both." She shakes Jena's and Mrs. Parker's hands. Then she walks off searching for Sam in the hallways. Jena and her mother walk out of the hospital to the car. They talk and laugh while walking to the car.

Mrs. Parker's cell phone rings. "It's your dad," she says.

"Mom, don't tell Dad yet," Jena pleads.

"Okay," Mrs. Parker replies and answers the phone. "Hi, honey. ... No, no, everything is all right. We're actually on our way home right now. ... Okay, I'll see you when we get there. ... "Love you too." Mrs. Parker winks at Jena. "I got him in the bag, but I do have to tell him everything. You do understand right?"

Jena smiles as she gets into the car. "Yes, Mom." Chance waves down the car as they are driving off. "Mom, it's Chance. Can you stop?" Jena asks.

Mrs. Parker stops the car. "Jena, did you see Jake?"

"Yes."

"What about Ken?"

"I just saw Jake; I didn't see Ken. I'm sorry," Jena says in a sad voice.

Chance suddenly becomes extremely upset. "I thought you were going to see how Ken was doing too!" Chance yells.

"Calm down, Chance," Jena replies. "I'm sure he's all right."

Chance runs away from the car and gets into her car where Carol is waiting and speeds away. Jena opens the door to get out and stop Chance. "Chance!" she yells. Jena stands in the parking lot and then slowly gets back into the car. "Hopefully, Ken's parents will let her see him." Jena closes the car door.

Mrs. Parker begins to drive home. She stops for an elderly couple walking to their car. On the way home, the main highway traffic is slowed down by a traffic jam. Police officers are directing traffic. Mrs. Parker drives slowly with the traffic. A car has flipped over a little further up the road.

"Mom, what do you think is going on?" Jena asks.

"There seems to be a car accident up ahead," Mrs. Parker replies. "Here comes a police officer. Maybe he can tell us what's going on."

"Hi, ma'am, there's been an accident, so please drive slowly as we try to get the injured individuals to the hospital. I'll be directing you past the accident. Please try to keep moving," the officer says.

"Thank you, Officer," Mrs. Parker replies. She drives slowly past the overturned car. Ambulances and police cars surround the accident area. Jena notices as their car passes that it's Chance's car.

"Mom! Mom! It's Chance. It's Chance and Carol!" Jena yells. "Stop the car, Mom!" Jena yells.

"Jena, I can't stop. I have to keep moving. You heard the officer," Mrs. Parker replies.

Jena stares out the car window in fear. The EMS team is carrying two people on stretchers to the ambulance. Jena's mother continues driving to their house.

CHAPTER SEVEN

"**M**om, what if something terrible has happened to Chance and Carol? I mean, what if they're really hurt or dead?"

"Jena, I'll try to contact Chance's mother. Both the girls were on stretchers. I mean, if they were dead, I'm sure we would have heard something by now."

"But, Mom!"

"Jena, calm down; you've had a rough day. First Jake and now these two girls. You need to just relax and take a deep breath."

"Okay." Jena breathes in deeply several times. She starts panicking again. "But, Mom, please try to call Chance's mother."

They both get out of car and walk into the house. Jena's father walks into the room. "What' going on? Cops are calling, and there's a car accident on the main highway that's got traffic backed the hell up!" Mr. Parker says in an angry voice.

Jena looks at her mom. Mrs. Parker looks at Jena. "Jena, go upstairs so I can speak to your father."

"Mom!" Jena whines.

"Jena, please, just go upstairs, so I can speak to your father. I promise I will let you know if I speak to Chance's mother."

"Okay, Mom." Jena walks slowly upstairs. She stops just at the top of the stairs to try to listen to what her parents are talking about.

Mr. Parker walks toward his wife. He gently grabs her arm and looks deeply into her eyes. "What's going, Kitty?" Mr. Parker asks.

Mrs. Parker walks toward the kitchen. She sighs. "Well, first, you might want to have a seat."

"Okay," Mr. Parker replies. He walks toward the couch and sits down. "So what's going on?" he asks again.

"Jena went to a club."

"A club? What kind of club?" Mr. Parker asks.

"It's not really a club; it's a biker bar."

Mr. Parker jumps up off the couch. "What?"

"Okay, calm down," Mrs. Parker says. "Let me explain. Apparently, Jena was just trying to make new friends with Chance and Carol."

"Who?" he replies.

"These two girls from school," Mrs. Parker says quickly. "They invited her to hang, just like girls do. They took her to this biker bar place, and things were going okay for while until Jake showed up."

"What the hell was Jake doing there?" Mr. Parker asks.

"Jake came by here earlier looking for Jena, and I told him that she wasn't home and that she left with two girls from school," she answers, sounding impatient.

"Okay," Mr. Parker replies. "I guess he knew where they were and went there."

"Ken was there too."

"Oh, I don't believe those two boys really like each other."

"Yes, that's true." Mrs. Parker nods her head yes. "Jake and Ken got into a fight, a real bad one, and now the both of them are in the hospital."

"Wow, now I can see why Jena is so upset," Mr. Parker says.

Mrs. Parker walks around the room in a circle. "One more thing," she says.

"There's more?" Mr. Parker replies.

"Yes, there's more," Mrs. Parker says sharply. "On our way home from the hospital, Chance and Carol were being escorted to the hospital in an ambulance. They are the ones that got into that car accident on the main highway. It appears they got into a car accident leaving the hospital." Mrs. Parker continues, "Chance left the hospital parking lot in spinning rage when Jena didn't have any information on how Ken was doing."

Mr. Parker looks up the stairs, and he notices Jena's shadow on the stairway. "Jena, come down stairs!" Mr. Parker calls. Jena stands frozen for moment. "Jena, come here. I can see you on the stairs."

Jena walks slowly down the stairs and stops on the last stair. "Dad, I'm sorry I didn't know all of this was going to happen today," Jena says slowly. "Please, don't be mad. I was just trying to make new friends, and I didn't know Jake was going to come or get into a fight."

Mr. Parker walks toward Jena. "It's okay, Jena. We're not blaming you for all of this." He gives her a hug. "I'm just a little shocked to hear about everything that happened today. I'm just very happy that you're not hurt." Mr. Parker gives Jena a bigger hug. "If something were to happen to you, Jena, I just don't know what I'd do. Jena, you are the only child I have." Mr. Parker squeezes her tightly and then turns to reach for Mrs. Parker's hand. "You and your mother …" He looks at Mrs. Parker with tears in his eyes. "You both are all I got."

"I know, Dad," Jena replies. "I decided that I want to be a volunteer at the hospital. I hope you will let me."

Mr. Parker turns to look as Mrs. Parker. She nods her head yes. "Well, if it's okay with your mom, then it's okay with me," Mr. Parker says. Jena gives her father a great big hug and runs upstairs. "Remember, everything I just said, Jena."

Jena stops at the top of the stairs. "I will, Dad. I promise." Jena walks to her room with a great big smile on her face. Her window is open. She walks slowly to it. The neighborhood streets are silent. She sees her next-door neighbor's cat roaming the neighborhood. She gets ready to go outside to get him when she hears a noise across the street. The living room light is on at the McNeils' house. Jena can see Mr. McNeil's shadow pacing back and forth in the living room. Mrs. McNeil is just standing still with her hand on her hip. Jena continues to stare curiously at the McNeils' shadows. Mr. McNeil walks toward Mrs. McNeil and grabs her neck. Jena stares with surprise. Mrs. McNeil is struggling to get loose. Mrs. McNeil raises her hand back and slaps Mr. McNeil in the face very hard. Mr. McNeil walks away quickly. Mrs. McNeil follows him and turns the living room lights off. Jena stands and leans over in her window surprised and shocked at what she has just witnessed. Jena hears another noise on the side of the McNeils' house. She looks harder to try to see what is moving in the dark. It is Mr. McNeil; he is standing next his house with a shovel in his hand. Jena tries to close her window quickly, but it is too late; Mr. McNeil looks up and sees her in the window. He stands still and stares at Jena. He smiles at her and then turns around to walk to his back door as he holds the shovel tightly gripped in his hand. Jena closes her bedroom window, puts on her pajamas, and tries to forget what she has just seen. Exhausted from the long day, Jena falls asleep quickly.

During the night, she tosses and turns in her sleep. *She begins to dream she is back on the plane. This time, she is the pilot. Jena dreams that she is flying the plane and all of the men on the plane are sitting silently. Jena makes an announcement to the male passengers aboard. "This is announcement from your pilot," she says. "I'm about to crash this airplane into the sea. Everyone, please stay calm and seated." The men on the airplane don't move. "Once I crash the plane, we are all going to die, so please buckle your seat belts and don't bother saying your prayers, because you're all creeps and you all deserve to die!" Jena flies the plane into the sea.*

She wakes up suddenly from the dream breathing hard and drenched in sweat. The morning sun is beaming through her window. *I wonder why Mom didn't wake me up,* she thinks. She hears a door close and two people talking and laughing outside. Jena runs to her window and sees Mr. and Mrs. McNeil kissing in their driveway. Jena rushes to get ready for school. She can smell the aroma of pancakes as it fills the room. She goes to the stairs and hears Mrs. Parker in the kitchen singing. Her mother's happy mood makes Jena feel at ease, but she is still confused by what she'd seen at the McNeils' house the night before—how just yesterday, they were such a happy couple, and then last night, he had a shovel in his hand like he was going to murder someone. Jena peeks out of her bedroom window. Kids are walking to school; the neighbor's dog is barking; and both of the McNeils' cars are in the driveway. *Maybe I was seeing things,* Jena thinks. *Maybe I'm just going crazy.*

CHAPTER EIGHT

Jena rushes down the stairs and slips on one of the steps on the way down. Mrs. Parker hurries out of the kitchen. "Jena, are you all right?" she asks.

Jena stumbles as she gets up. "Yes, Mom, you know, clumsy me," Jena answers.

"Well, next time, be careful. You know your dad's been meaning to repair those darn stairs. You could get hurt if you're not careful."

Jena walks to the kitchen door. "Mom, I'm sorry; I'm going to have to skip breakfast this morning. I had another bad night's sleep, and I'm running late," Jena says in a hurry.

"But, honey, I made all of your favorites," Mrs. Parker says in a whiny voice. "Jena, just sit down and have a few bites, and I'll take you to school," she insists.

"Okay, Mom," Jena says as she sits down at the kitchen table. She starts eating breakfast, and Mr. Parker comes downstairs.

He sits at the table next to Jena and Mrs. Parker and opens up the morning newspaper. "Aren't you supposed to be getting along to school, young lady?" he says.

Jena looks up at her dad with sad, sleepy eyes.

"She's running a little late this morning; you know, bad night's sleep again," Mrs. Parker says, "I'm going to be taking her to school today. After all of the excitement from yesterday, I can understand how Jena might not sleep well."

Mr. Parker raises one of his eyebrows at Mrs. Parker. Jena quickly finishes her breakfast. "Well, Mom, we better get going."

Looking down at her watch, her mom says, "You're right, Jena. It is getting late." Mrs. Parker grabs her purse and car keys, and Jena grabs her book bag. Mrs. Parker leans over and gives Mr. Parker a kiss on the cheek. "Now, you be good today," she says with a smile.

Jena walks quickly to the front door. Mr. Parker turns around from the kitchen table. "Ah, Jena, no kiss for Dad?"

"Dad, you know I'm not a little kid anymore," Jena replies.

"Just kidding, honey, but every once in awhile, you can at least give your old dad a hug." Mr. Parker smiles as he turns back around to read his paper. Jena goes back to the kitchen and hugs her dad, and then she and Mrs. Parker head to the car. Mrs. Parker backs out of her driveway just as a delivery truck is passing by. The delivery truck almost collides with Mrs. Parker's car. She stops quickly. The delivery driver gets out of his truck. He walks with a limp, and it takes him a few seconds to get to the car. Mrs. Parker is in a rush, so she blows her horn. The delivery driver walks up and taps on her window.

"Are you all right, ma'am?" he mumbles.

Mrs. Parker rolls down the car window. "Yes. Sorry, I didn't see you," Mrs. Parker says.

"It's all right, ma'am. I believe it was my fault. I wasn't paying attention like I should, but please don't call the boss."

Jena and Mrs. Parker look at each other. The delivery driver leans over to look at Jena. "I'm just glad you and the young lady are all right," he says. Trying to make conversation with Jena, he asks, "So what's your name, young lady?"

Mrs. Parker answers quickly, "I'm Mrs. Parker, and she is Jena. I'm so sorry, sir, but we are in such a rush."

"Oh, sure, sure," he answers. "It was nice meeting the both of you, and you two have a good day now, you hear?" The delivery driver limps back to his truck and continues driving down the street. Mrs. Parker backs out of her driveway and begins driving Jena to school.

"Mom, that was a close call. He was a strange one, wouldn't you say?" Jena says.

"Yeah, it was. There must be something in this town that spurs car accidents," Mrs. Parker replies.

"Mom, remember you have to pick me up today so I can start my first day as a hospital volunteer."

"Oh yeah! Today is the big day for you to somewhat start a job."

Jena and her mother both laugh.

"And of course you get to see Jake." Mrs. Parker turns and looks at Jena.

"I hope he's all right, Mom."

"I'm sure he's doing well, Jena."

"He's my best friend, and I still feel a little responsible for what happened at that club," Jena replies.

"Jena, it wasn't your fault." Mrs. Parker continues to drive. "I'm sure Jake didn't want to get into a fight, but he did and he has to take responsibility for that. I know he didn't mean to get hurt, but Jake knew that he and Ken haven't gotten along since middle school, so maybe he should have left the bar or not have gone at all."

"Mom, Jake and I have been friends since grade school. You know he's like a brother to me. I know he was just trying to protect me," Jena replies. "I mean, I don't really like Ken either, but he's Chance's boyfriend, and I couldn't exactly ignore him at the club, although I wish I had now," Jena says as she puts her head down.

Mrs. Parker pulls up at the school. "Jena, I know Jake is your friend, but are you sure that something else isn't going on there?" she asks.

"Yes, Mom, nothing." Jena opens the car door and closes it. She leans over into the passenger's car window. "Don't forget to come pick me up after school," she says to her mother.

"I won't," Mrs. Parker replies.

Jena smiles at her mom, throws her book bag over her shoulder, and walks toward the school. Other students are standing around everywhere, and everyone is whispering as Jena passes them. One student stops Jena. "Hey, aren't you the girl who got in a fight at that club last night?"

Jena keeps walking. Another student stops her. "Jena, did Jake really get knocked out? I heard that Ken knocked his ass out, and then Ken got stabbed by the bouncer. Is that what happened?" the kid asks.

"No!" Jena replies harshly. She continues to walk to her locker. Ken's brother Ted stands next to Jena in the hallway.

"Jena!" Ted calls.

Jena turns. "Ted, how is Ken?" she asks. "I'm sorry about what happened to him and Jake. I didn't want anyone to get hurt."

"I know, Jena, it's not your fault," Ted replies. "I know my brother isn't innocent, although my parents think he's a saint. Don't worry; Ken is doing okay. He's still a little banged up, but I think he'll live. I also heard that Jake is doing okay too," he says.

"Yeah, I think Jake will be all right," Jena replies. "What about Chance and Carol?" she asks.

Ted moves closer to Jena. "Well, I heard that Carol is in real bad shape, but Chance is doing okay," Ted replies.

"How bad is Carol?" Jena asks. "What do you mean?"

"Not physical, but mental. She's upset about something. Who knows what's going on with her?" Ted says. "I just can't believe that everyone is in the hospital in this town. It almost feels like we're living in a cursed town. Maybe we're in the Twilight Zone, huh, Jena," Ted adds as he backs away to go to class. "My parents are pissed, not at Ken, but at me for not being there to stop the fight. Can you believe that? You know, my dad being a preacher and all, this type of news isn't good for the church." Ted backs into a group of Ken's teammates.

"Hey, Ted, so how's Ken doing?" Bobby, one of Ken's hangout buddies asks. Several of the other guys glance over at Jena. "He's doing well. I gotta go," Ted replies quickly.

Bobby glares at Jena from the corner of his eye to make sure she is paying attention. "It's too bad that Ken didn't kick Jake's ass a little harder." Bobby smirks at Jena.

Ted gets in his face. "Look, man, what's too bad is that either of them got hurt fighting just to see who's got the bigger head when I can clearly see you do," Ted says.

"Yeah?" the guy replies.

"Yeah," Ted says.

One of Ken's other teammates pulls on the guy's arm, and they all walk away. Ted turns to Jena. "Jena, don't worry about those jerks."

"I won't." She slams her locker door and walks to her classroom. Talking to herself, she says, "I just want everyone to get out of the hospital."

Ted catches up with her. "Ted, we better go to class, or we're going to be late, and you know how Mr. Jamison gets when we're late for his class." Before walking into the classroom, she adds, "Hey, Ted, after school, I'm going to volunteer at the hospital. Hopefully, I'll get to see everyone while I'm there." They both take their seats in the class.

The school day goes by very quickly for Jena. The last school bell rings, and she rushes outside to wait for her mother. Ken's teammates are all standing around laughing, joking, and staring at her. She ignores them and sits down on the bench outside the school building. Jena opens a book and begins to read. A delivery truck pulls up, and it's the same guy who almost got into an accident with her mom that morning. The deliveryman gets out and limps toward the school. He notices Jena on the bench and walks up to her. "Hey, aren't you the young lady from this morning?" he asks.

Jena looks up slowly. The sun is shining in her eyes. "Yes, I am," she answers reluctantly.

The delivery driver stands over Jena blocking half of the sun behind him. Jena begins to feel uncomfortable. She stands and pretends she is looking for her mother. The delivery driver moves closer to her. "You're a pretty young lady," he says.

Jena moves away from him and notices her mother. She grabs her things and quickly walks toward her mother's car. The delivery driver just stands and stares as she walks away. "Hey!" he yells.

Jena slowly turns around and stands in a frozen state. He limps over to Jena holding one of her books in his hand. Jena watches as he slowly limps toward her. She prays that he will move a little faster, but for some reason, she just can't move herself.

"You forgot your book."

Jena slowly reaches for her book. The driver smiles; his teeth are crooked and dirty. He hands Jena the book. Jena looks at him and swallows. "Thank you," she says quietly and then turns away quickly. Mrs. Parker begins blowing the car horn.

The delivery driver yells, "And by the way, my name is Joe! Joe Johnson! It was nice to meet ya!" He lowers his voice and adds, "And I'll see you again, I hope."

CHAPTER NINE

Jena gets into the car. She looks back at the delivery driver, who is still standing near the bench staring at her. Mrs. Parker begins driving away.

"So how was your day?" Mrs. Parker asks.

Jena doesn't answer. She is preoccupied with the delivery driver.

"Jena, did you hear me?"

"Yeah, Mom. Today was fine," she replies.

Mrs. Parker drives to the hospital. Jena gets out. "Call me, Jena, when you're almost done," Mrs. Parker says.

"I will, Mom, and thanks again." Jena walks into the hospital.

An emergency situation is going on as she walks through the door. She goes to Ms. Louis's office to pick up her uniform and to find out which floor she will be working on for the day. Jena walks into Ms. Louis's office. Ms. Louis is scanning her computer screen. She looks up. "Hi, Jena. Welcome to your first day as a hospital volunteer," she says.

Ms. Louis appears to be in a rush. She hands Jena her uniform. "Well, here's your new outfit," she jokes. Jena takes her uniform. "You will report to Ms. Cook, who will be your supervisor for today. She is located on the second floor. So do you have any questions?" she asks.

Jena shakes her head no. "Well then, good luck." Ms. Louis rushes out of her office, giving Jena a quick wave. Jena walks out behind her. She goes to the elevator door. The door opens, and she sees a man inside. Jena walks into the elevator. No one but the man is in the elevator. He is silent. Jena steps into the elevator, and then the door closes. The man reaches for the number two button. Jena stands back feeling a little frightened. The elevator door opens to the second floor. She looks back at the elevator. The tall suited man is still there. She sighs with relief. The elevator door closes. She walks to the nurses' station. A nurse is sitting at the computer looking over what appears to be notes on a chart.

"Excuse me?" Jena speaks softly. "My name is Jena, Jena Parker, and I'm looking for Ms. Cook."

The nurse points to her name tag. "I'm Ms. Cook, and I'm assuming you're my volunteer for today."

"Yes, ma'am."

She looks at Jena with wide eyes and one hand on her hip. "Well then, go change into your work clothes. Come back, and I'll tell you what to do." Jena changes and then returns with her clothes in her hand. "You can put those in a locker in the back," Ms. Cook says.

Jena does so and returns again. "Now, the first thing I would like you to do is to go to each room on this floor and visit the patient. Ask each patient if there is anything they need." Ms. Cook sits downs and begins working on her computer as she is giving Jena instructions.

"Yes, ma'am," Jena replies.

She walks down the hall to the first patient's room. The door is closed. Jena opens the door slowly. The patient is turned on his side. "Sir, my name is Jena, and I'd like to see if there is anything I can do for you today?"

The patient turns over. It is Ken. Jena is surprised. "Hi, Jena," Ken says slowly, in a low, raspy voice.

Jena walks closer to Ken's bedside. "Ken, how're you doing?"

"Oh, I'm doing all right, I guess," Ken replies trying not to look directly at her. "I'm getting stronger every day."

"Well, that's great." Jena sits down in the chair next to Ken's bed. "I'm glad you're doing well," she says.

"Yeah, I think I'll be getting out of the hospital real soon," Ken replies. "So what are you doing here dressed like that?" Ken asks.

Jena tugs at her shirt. "I'm a volunteer," she replies.

Ken smirks a little. "A volunteer? Here at the hospital?" He looks at her in disbelief. Then he turns away. "You volunteered to see Jake, didn't you? I heard he's in a room right down the hall from me," Ken says in an angry voice.

"He is," Jena answers with excitement.

"Yes, well, don't let me hold you up."

Jena stands up from the chair. "Ken, I'm really sorry about what happened," she says. "I didn't mean for you or Jake to fight. I certainly didn't think you guys would take it this far."

"Yeah, well, shit happens," Ken replies.

Jena shakes her head and begins walking out of Ken's room. She turns around. "Ken, did you know that Chance and Carol are in the hospital too?"

Ken tries to sit up in his bed. "What happened to them, Jena?"

"On the way home yesterday, my mom and I saw a car accident. It was Chance and Carol. I believe Chance was upset, because I guess your mom wouldn't let her see you and I went to visit Jake, but I didn't get any information about you, so she was mad."

Ken remains quiet. Jena moves closer to him and touches his hand. "But I'm here to check on the both of you today." Ken squeezes her hand.

"Damn, why is everything so messed up right now? I have to find out where she is!" Ken says in a concerned voice. "Jena, please tell me when you find out anything else about what's going on."

"Sure, I will."

Jena walks out of Ken's hospital room. She continues down the hallway looking in every room trying to locate Jake. He isn't where he was last night. She finally finds him in the last room down the hall. Jake's room door is open, and he is watching a football game. Jena walks in, and Jake smiles at her. "Look at you. You're a candy striper, right?" Jake says in a joking voice.

"Very funny, it's called a hospital volunteer outfit," Jena replies.

"Oh, that's what they call it now? You look like an oversized candy cane."

Jena walks closer to Jake's bed. He starts laughing again. Jena stops and looks around the room. "I'm glad you're so happy. Don't laugh too hard; you may break your stitches or I may cause you to get more."

Jake laughs again. "That's why I love you, Jena." An awkward silence fills the room.

"Ah," Jena replies. Trying to change the subject, she says, "So is there anything I can get you? Anything you need?"

"Yes, you can get me the hell out of here; I'm bored to death," Jake replies.

Trying to fix Jake's pillow, Jena says, "You know I can't do that, Jake, but what I can do is get you something to drink or maybe another pillow?"

Jake sits up in his bed. He stares at Jena with a serious look on his face. "How about you come over and give me a kiss? That'll make me feel better."

"Jake, I think you really are sick. Why are you talking this way? I know you think you're okay, but you still need rest," Jena says. "Stop joking around. What's gotten into you lately?"

Jake has a serious look on his face. "I'm not joking, Jena. I'm serious. There is something I have been wanting to tell you for a long time now, but I just couldn't," Jake says.

Jena stops and stands still with an uncertain look on her face. "Jake, don't."

"No, Jena, I have to. I have to tell you now. First, please sit down. If I don't tell you now, I may never tell you. Jena, I know we have been friends since kindergarten." Jake pauses and then reaches for Jena's hand. "We're in high school now, and ever since the eighth grade, I've had these feelings for you. This is crazy, I know," Jake says in a shy voice. "Jena, I love you."

Jena moves her hand away from Jake's. "What?" she responds, surprised.

"I love you," Jake says again in a more confident voice. "You're my best friend, and I love you so much. I know I love you, because you're all I think about. That's why I went so crazy when I saw Ken's arms around you—that and the fact that I can't stand him. It drove me crazy to see him touching you. That's why I reacted the way I did. I was out of my head." Jake licks his lips. "It was weird, but all I wanted to do was kill him."

Jena stands up from the chair. She walks toward the door and then turns around. Tears begin to flow from her eyes. She opens the door. "Jena, don't go." She stops with the door in her hand, halfway open. "Jena, please don't go." She walks out and closes the door gently behind her. She walks slowly down the hospital halls with her arms folded and tears flowing. She goes to the women's bathroom where she stands and stares at herself in the mirror. Tears run down her cheeks. The reflection changes in the mirror, and for a split second, she looks evil and angry.

"Who are you?" she asks herself. The reflection of herself smiles back at her. She passes out. When she awakes, she is on the floor facedown. Her legs are crooked, and she has scraped her knee on a piece of broken tile on the floor. Her knee is bleeding slightly. She gets up and splashes water on her face, cleans her knee, and then leans closer to look in the mirror again.

"What are you, and who are you?" she whispers.

CHAPTER TEN

The dark illusion in the mirror lightens again. She continues to stare at herself. Her tears stop. She gently splashes water on her face again and then takes a paper towel to dry it. She walks back toward Jake's room, but there is a nurse in his room. Jena stands and watches through the room door's narrow window. Jake leans over and stares back at her. He smiles. She smiles back at him and then places her hand on the glass to signal to him that she is all right. She turns and goes to complete her welcome rounds with other patients. Jena heads back in the direction of the nurses' station to check in with Nurse Cook. Nurse Cook appears preoccupied with responding to patient requests and out-of-control room buzzers. Jena walks up to the counter. Nurse Cook is overwhelmed.

"Jena, I need to go to the fourth floor to room 406 to check on a patient who is buzzing every five seconds. She has been buzzing me for the last few minutes, but I can't leave the nurses' station." Feeling overwhelmed, she says, "They all have been buzzing."

"Okay, Ms. Cook, I'll go straight there." Jena rushes to the elevator, pushes the button, and waits. The elevator seems to be stuck on the first floor. Jena looks around for the hospital staircase. Opening the stairway exit door, she finds the stairway is empty and creepy. Jena walks up to the fourth floor to room 406; the door is cracked open and the room dark. Jena can hear a girl crying.

"Hello?" Jena says as she slowly opens the door. "My name is Jena, and I'm a hospital volunteer. I'm here to help you." Jena reaches for the light switch. "I'm just going to turn on the light, so I can see you," she says softly.

The girl tries to speak through her tears. "Don't turn on the lights!" she says in a voice harsh from crying.

Jena slowly steps back toward the room door. "Hi, I'm not sure if you heard me, but my name is Jena. I'm here to help you."

"Jena, is that you?" the girl asks.

Jena recognizes the voice. "Carol?" she replies.

"Yes, it's me, Carol."

Jena slowly walks toward Carol's bedside. She sits on a chair next to her. "Carol, it's dark in here. Why do you want the lights off?"

"No! No lights!" Carol screams. "I like crying in the dark." She snuffles. "I know it sounds crazy, but crying in the dark makes me feel better."

"Carol, I'm so sorry for what happened to you and Chance. I saw you guys on the highway. You were on stretchers. Why are you crying?" Jena asks. "What's wrong?" Jena looks around the dark room. "Besides being here in the hospital."

"Jena, I've been friends with Chance for a long time, but there's something I haven't told her, something I haven't told anyone." Carol turns around in her bed. "Jena, turn on the bed's overhead light? It's not as bright." Jena turns on the light and sits back down. Carol's eyes are red and puffy. Carol reaches for Jena's hand. She has a serious look on her face. "Jena, I'm in love with Ken." Jena shifts in her chair. She doesn't say anything. Carol squeezes her hand. "I'm in love with Ken, and Ken's in love with me, I know it. We have been secretly seeing each other behind Chance's back for over a year now. I don't know what to do. He's hurt, and he won't speak to me. I went down to his room, and he wouldn't even look at me. You're the only person I have told about my true feelings for Ken." Jena sits in silence and continues to listen to Carol. Carol sits up in her bed and raises her voice. "I mean, do you have any idea what it is like to be in love with someone who thinks they're in love with someone else?"

Jena has a stunned look on her face. "Carol, I …" Jena stops. "I don't know what to say. I haven't known you and Chance that long, but you two seem like very close friends. Maybe you should just tell her."

Carol begins to cry a little. "I can't tell her." She gives Jena a weird look. "This is why I'm telling you. I have to talk to someone about this. Just promise me, Jena, promise me you won't tell Chance or Jake. Please," Carol pleads. "This is has been very hard for me."

Not sure if she should keep the secret, Jena tells Carol what she wants to hear. "I promise, Carol, but you shouldn't be worried about them right now," Jena says. "You should be concentrating on getting better. I'm volunteering at the hospital for a while. Is there anything you need right now?"

Looking away, she says, "No. ... Yes." Carol changes her mind. "I need Ken, but I know you can't do anything for me." Carol leans back down in her bed. She curls her arm under her head and pillow. "Jena, do you know what it's like to love someone who doesn't even notice you? Someone you know may never love you the same way?" Jena thinks about Jake. "Jena, I love Ken so much that sometimes I think I could die for him. Having to my hide my feelings hurts so much inside. I'm so tired of pretending." Sounding delusional, she continues, "I want to be with the man I love!" Carol starts to cry again. Jena just sits quietly while Carol sheds tears of pain. She thinks back to just moments earlier when Jake confessed his love to her and how she couldn't tell Jake she loved him back because she wasn't sure of her feelings. Carol continues to cry, and Jena continues to think about Jake. Carol stops crying and notices Jena is thinking to herself. Feeling sorry for Jena, she says, "Jena, I can tell that you will find an incredible love someday. This person will love you so much that it will overwhelm you," Carol says.

Jena stands up and leans over to Carol with a sad, grim look on her face. "Carol, I know it must hurt you to love a person who is in love with someone else. I'm sorry you have to pretend that you don't, but you have to ask yourself if it's really worth it. Is it worth it for you to lose yourself when you're so young?"

Carol looks away from Jena in disappointment. "Jena, please leave!" she screams.

Jena nods her head and begins walking out of the room. She stands by the door for a second and then opens it and walks out. She walks slowly down the hospital hallway. Carol starts screaming very loudly, "I love him!" She screams over and over again, but Jena just keeps walking.

A nurse stops Jena in the hallway. "What's going on? What's wrong with that patient?"

Jena stares at the nurse. "She's heartbroken," she replies. Jena can't believe the sudden change in herself; she feels no compassion for Carol. She stares at the nurse again. "And you can't heal a heartbroken person when they don't want to be healed," Jena says as she walks down the hallway. The nurse just looks at Jena strangely and then rushes off to Carol's room.

Jena takes the elevator back down to the first floor to Ms. Louis's office. She is sitting in her office reviewing paperwork. Jena stands in the doorway. Ms. Louis looks up from her computer and notices Jena standing near her office door. She stands up from her chair and puts the paper down on her desk. "Jena, is something wrong?" Jena just stands with a blank look on her face. Ms. Louis walks over to her and grabs her shoulders. "Jena, can you speak? Did something happen with one of the patients?" Ms. Louis asks.

Jena looks at Ms. Louis with a lost look on her face. "I don't think I can do this job, Ms. Louis." She starts to shake. "I don't think I'm cut out to be a hospital volunteer."

Ms. Louis walks Jena into her office and sits her down. "Jena, not everyone is meant to do this job," she replies. "This job certainly requires a strong and willing individual who is open to all that can occur in a hospital. Some people have physical, mental, and social needs. You're just starting out; give it some time." Ms. Louis sits back down at her desk. "Let me try to explain to you why I became a nurse." Jena sits quietly in the chair waiting to hear Ms. Louis tell her story. "Jena, when I was a young lady, I sat and watched while my mother struggled with cancer. We were poor, and she couldn't afford to go to the hospital all the time or seek medical treatment every single time she got sick. I remember my mother working all day and then coming home tired and sick. She would vomit blood and lay still on the bathroom floor for hours. Even as a young child, it was painful to watch. After she'd lay there for hours, she would get up, take a shower, and still make dinner. I grew up watching her struggle with this disease; yet she was the strongest woman I've known. My mother died when I was fifteen, and my brother and I ended up going to stay with my aunt and uncle. They were nice people, but it wasn't the same as having my mother's love and comfort. My father wasn't a part of our lives, so she was all we had. When I was seventeen, my brother was shot in the chest." Ms. Louis begins to cry. "Right in front of me. I felt hopeless and helpless in trying to save his life. I screamed for help, but in the neighborhood we lived in, no one cared. He died in my arms. Blood was everywhere, and I was so angry and hurt that I'd lost the only two people I truly loved. The day my brother was buried, I saw a young girl dressed as a hospital volunteer. That is when it hit me, what I wanted to do. So I also became a volunteer for a local hospital. Since that time, I've seen many deaths and many happy outcomes for patients who had severe illnesses. Both moments have had an impact on my life, which has made me a better person inside and in a lot of ways healed me from my mother's and brother's deaths. I understand now that being a nurse is not just saving lives and healing people's bodies, but also their spirits. So you see, Jena, this is my reason for being a nurse.

You have to ask yourself what's yours? Becoming a nurse is not always something you choose to do, but something that chooses you."

Jena looks up at the room's ceiling and then back at Ms. Louis and smiles. "I can do this." Jena sits up straight in the chair. "Maybe I can't be you, but I certainly can try." Ms. Louis stands up and gives Jena a big hug. Jena smiles with confidence. "Well, I better get back to work before Ms. Cook calls down here looking for me," Jena says.

"Jena, why don't you just go home for the day? Think about what I said, and then if you still want to be a volunteer, come back tomorrow. Call your mother to pick you up, go home, think, and then come back tomorrow," Ms. Louis says. "I realize that you have a lot going on in your life. You're about to graduate, possibly go to college, and you have several friends who have unfortunately ended up in the hospital recently." Ms. Louis smiles a little. "That could raise anyone's blood pressure. I'll speak to Ms. Cook. What we spoke about here today is just between us."

"Okay … Okay," Jena replies. Jena walks out of Ms. Louis's office; she sits outside on the hospital bench and takes her cell phone out to call her mother. "Mom, I'm done for the day. Could you come pick me up?" Jena asks.

Jena hangs up and waits for her mother to pick her up. The hospital's automatic doors open, and Mr. McNeil emerges. He has a hold of a woman's arm, and he seems angry. The woman has a paper in her hand. He lets her go, and she waives the paper in his face and then slaps him. Jena can't hear what they are saying, but she notices that they are having a really serious argument. The woman throws the paper in Mr. McNeil's face and walks off quickly. Mr. McNeil picks the paper up from off the ground, crumbles it up, lights up a cigarette, and then walks to his car in the parking lot. Jena sits still on the bench, confused about what she just saw happen between Mr. McNeil and a woman who isn't his wife. Mr. McNeil throws his cigarette down on the ground, gets into his car, and slams the door. He drives past the hospital doors and notices Jena sitting on the bench. He stops his car, gets out, and walks up to Jena.

"What did you see?" Mr. McNeil asks. Jena sits frozen on the bench. He speaks to her in an angry voice. "I said, 'What did you see?'"

Mrs. Parker drives up and sticks her head out the car window. "Hi, Miles. Come on, Jena. Let's go. I'm in a rush. Dinner is on the stove."

Mr. McNeil turns around quickly, trying to change the angry expression on his face. "Hello, Kitty." Mrs. Parker gives him a strange look. Feeling guilty, he adds, "Oh, I'm just getting some results, but nothing to worry about." Mr. McNeil fixes his toupee. Jena stands up and rushes to get into her mother's car. Mrs. Parker drives off, and Mr. McNeil waves at them. Jena watches out of the passenger's side mirror as the car is driving away. Mr. McNeil is standing near the bench and staring at the car as it drives away. Jena sits in the car scared to death.

CHAPTER ELEVEN

Jena sits quietly in the car while Mrs. Parker goes on and on about how badly her day went, starting from when the trash truck almost hit Mr. Chester's dog. An old lady, Ms. Barber, went missing for a few hours because of her Alzheimer's disease. Mrs. Parker keeps talking, but Jena zones out. She tunes in for a moment just in time to catch her mother saying, "Can you believe everyone in the neighborhood was searching for her and she was sitting in her backyard the whole time? Not to mention that your grandma keeps calling me to come see her."

Jena zones out again. She flashes back to her dream when she was on the airplane with all those unknown men. She thinks back to when she saw Mr. and Mrs. McNeil arguing that one day and then them making up as if nothing had happened, and now this strange encounter when she caught Mr. McNeil arguing with an unknown woman? Who was that woman? *What a strange thing to see,* Jena thinks. Mr. McNeil seemed so different when he saw her watching him and that woman. He was mean and scary. He was still creepy, but something in his actions made Jena feel fearful of him. Interrupting her mom's bad-day sermon, she says, "Mom?"

Mrs. Parker pauses. She turns toward Jena slightly. "Do you think that Mr. McNeil acts strange sometimes?" Jena asks.

Mrs. Parker leans back in her seat. "I've known Miles since high school," she answers. "He always made me wonder; that's all I can say. Jena, why would you ask such a strange question?" Jena doesn't reply. "Did he say or do something to you, Jena?"

"Never mind, Mom," Jena says.

Mrs. Parker shrugs Jena's strange question off. Silence fills the car. Trying to break the silence, she says, "He's an all right person, Jena, except when you get trapped in a conversation with him, and then that's when you're doomed." Jena laughs a little. Then the both of them burst out in laughter. Mrs. Parker pulls up in the driveway. Mrs. McNeil is already home and is standing by her car talking on her cell phone. Jena and Mrs. Parker peek over at her as she waves her hand and paces angrily up and down the driveway. Jena wonders if Mrs. McNeil is angry because she knows something? She looks back on how Mr. McNeil was so quick to approach her after she caught him with the unknown woman. Mrs. McNeil is crying and screaming on her cell phone. "How could you do this to me?" she screams. "You said you would never do this again!" she screams even louder.

Jena and Mrs. Parker sit in the car and listen. "I should go and check on her," Mrs. Parker suggests with concern. Mrs. McNeil goes on and on, screaming and yelling at the caller, and then she throws the phone in the backyard and walks into the house. She slams the door. Mrs. Parker gets out of the car. "I'm going over there; she seems really mad."

Mrs. Parker walks over to Mrs. McNeil's house. She knocks on the door and calls out for Mrs. McNeil, but she doesn't answer. Jena stands and watches while her mother tries to get Mrs. McNeil to open the door. Mrs. Parker walks back toward her house. Jena is outside the car looking curiously with her bag hanging off one shoulder. Mrs. Parker walks toward her. "She won't open the door."

"Mom!" Jena calls. Mrs. Parker passes her. "Do think she'll be all right? What do you think is going on?" Jena asks.

Mrs. Parker just shakes her head and walks toward the house. Jena follows her into the house and sits down on the couch. Mrs. Parker walks into the kitchen. Jena puts her hands over her face and rubs her eyes, and then she stands up and peeks out the living room window to see if Mrs. McNeil has come back to get her phone. Jena opens the front door. The wind is blowing hard, neighborhood kids are playing in the street, and there is no sign of Mrs. McNeil outside. Mr. McNeil pulls into his driveway. Jena closes the front door quickly. Mrs. Parker is starting dinner in the kitchen and doesn't notice Jena peeking outside. Mr. McNeil gets out of the car and strolls to the house. His work briefcase is swinging in one hand, and he has a dozen roses in the other. Mr. McNeil puts his key in the doorway, but Mrs. McNeil has already opened the door. They began to argue in the doorway. Mrs. McNeil pushes him outside as he tries to push his way into the house. He hands her the flowers, but she snatches them out of his hand and throws them out the front door. Mr. McNeil continues to try to force his way into the house. He pushes her as he struggles to get through the front door. Jena can no longer see Mrs. McNeil, only Mr. McNeil standing in the doorway with his briefcase lifted up as if he were going to hit her. He turns to look to see if anyone is watching him, and then he slams the front door. Jena watches with her mouth open. She grips the living room curtain watching as she waits to see what happens next, but she can't see any movement in the house. She runs upstairs to peek out her bedroom window. She stands there for at least a half hour. Night begins to fall, but she continues to stand there, peeking out the window hoping to get a glimpse of something. As the dark moves in, there are still no lights on at the McNeils' house.

Mrs. Parker walks into Jena's room. "Jena, why are you standing by the window?"

Jena is startled. She turns around and then smiles at her mother. She lies. "Oh, I was just watching the kids playing out in the street. I was just caught up in the moment, remembering what it was like when I was a kid and played outside all night long. Do you remember that, Mom?"

Mrs. Parkers walks up to Jena's window. She lightly moves Jena's curtain back. "Of course I remember," she replies. "How I could I forget." She turns around to pat Jena on the shoulder and then continues to peek out of the window. "No lights are on," she whispers to herself as she peeks out the window concerned about her longtime friend Jane McNeil. She wonders why Jane doesn't turn on any lights in the house when both cars are parked in the driveway.

"Jena, did you see Jane and Miles leave with someone else?" Trying to rationalize the situation, she adds, "Maybe they went to dinner with the Carsons." She stands and stares out the window. Jena is silent. Mrs. Parkers turns to look at her.

Jena has a blank look on her face, and then she lies to her mother.

"No, Mom, all I saw was the kids."

Mrs. Parker walks out of Jena's room and back downstairs. She stops and peeks out the living room window. Her obsession with finding out what is going on is growing. She stands and watches the McNeils' house. Car headlights turn the corner into their driveway. Mr. Parker gets out of the car and walks into the house. Mrs. Parker has a sad look on her face. Mr. Parker walks up to her. "What's wrong, Kitty?" He grabs her and pulls her close to him. He sits her down on the couch.

"Ah, I'm just worried about Jane. She and Miles had a fight again. I hope she is all right."

Mr. Parker peeks out the window. "Well, it looks like Miles is home, but I don't see any lights on in the house. Maybe I should go over there to see what's going on."

Mrs. Parker stands up. "No, honey, don't go over there," she replies. "Maybe they just need a little time alone."

Mr. Parker hugs Mrs. Parker. "Maybe we need a little time alone." He kisses her. "Is Jena home?"

Mrs. Parker starts giggling. "Yes, she's upstairs," she whispers.

"Well then, we are just going to have to be quiet," Mr. Parker says playfully.

"You bad boy," Mrs. Parker replies. "Let's just wait until Jena goes to sleep."

They both giggle. A light finally comes on at the McNeils'.

"Kitty, the lights just came on," Mr. Parker says. He walks over to the window. Mr. McNeil's shadow is pacing back in forth in the living room window. Mrs. Parker joins him at the window. They both stand and stare through their window and watch Mr. McNeil pace back and forth.

"What do you think is wrong with him?" Mrs. Parker asks.

"I don't know, Kit." He gives Kitty a concerned look. "Do you think I should go over there?" he asks again. Mr. Parker begins pacing. "I think I should go over there," he says.

Mrs. Parker is silent for a moment. "Ah, I don't know," she replies reluctantly. "I tried to speak to Jane earlier, but she wouldn't open the door. Maybe we should let them work it out."

Mr. Parker turns and walks around the room. "I don't know, Kitty," he says in an uncertain voice.

"This looks like something serious. I know you're concerned," Mrs. Parker says. "I am too, but you know those two have been at it since we were in high school. I'm sure they'll find a way to work it out."

"Yeah, you're right," Mr. Parker replies. "So what's for dinner?" he asks.

Smiling, she answers, "I was making your favorite today."

A surprised look crosses his face. "Really?" Mr. Parker runs to the kitchen. "You made meatloaf?"

"No," Mrs. Parker says, "because just when I was getting ready to make dinner, Jena called. So I ran out and picked her up, and dinner is not ready yet." Mrs. Parker taps Mr. Parker on the shoulder. "Besides, you're home early today, so you'll just have to wait." Mrs. Parker walks to the kitchen and removes a pan from the kitchen cabinet. Mr. Parker just stands in the living room still peeking out the window at the McNeils'. Mrs. Parker yells from the kitchen. "And I'm not making meatloaf, because it'll take too long."

Peeking out the window again, Mr. Parker answers, "Uh-huh."

Mrs. Parker yells from the kitchen again, "I'm just going to make some beans and rice!"

Still distracted by Mr. McNeil's pacing shadow, Mr. Parker answers slowly, "Okay, hon, anything you make is fine with me."

Jena is still upstairs staring at the McNeils' house from her room's window. She pulls a chair up from her desk, turns off her lights, and then sits down to stare at the McNeils' house. She peeks through her window as if she were a spy. Mr. McNeil is still pacing back and forth. Jena stares at the McNeils' house for an hour. He paces back and forth, but now, he has something in his hand.

Mrs. Parker calls for Jena, "Jena, time for dinner!"

Jena is mesmerized by the McNeils'. She doesn't want to leave the window. Mrs. Parker yells again, "Jena, dinner!"

Jena quickly turns on her room lights, puts her chair back, and then runs downstairs. She walks into the kitchen. Mr. Parker is sitting at the table reading a newspaper. "So, Mom, what's for dinner?" Jena asks.

Mr. Parker looks up from the paper. "Beans and rice," he says in a disappointed voice.

Mrs. Parker gives him a mean look. "You said you didn't care."

He smiles at Mrs. Parker and begins reading his paper again. Jena sits down at the table. "I like beans and rice, Mom."

Mr. Parker puts his paper down. "I like beans and rice too, but I pay a terrible price later."

Mrs. Parker laughs. She turns off the stove. There is a knock at the door. Mr. Parker puts his paper down and goes to open it. Jake is leaning in the doorway. "Hi, sir. Is Jena around?" Jake asks.

Jena hears Jake's voice and, surprised, stands up from the kitchen table and walks toward the front door.

CHAPTER TWELVE

Jake leans over in the door, gripping the door-knob tightly. "Jake, what are you doing here?"

Jake leans further in the doorway. He walks into the house. "I came here to see you. I wanted to know how you were doing."

Mr. Parker gently grabs Jake's arm to help him into the house. He walks Jake slowly to the couch. Jake puts his hand on his forehead. "Jake, are you all right?" Jena reaches over to him.

He looks up at her. "Now I am," he says with that smile he always gives Jena. Mr. Parker smiles a little himself and walks back into the kitchen.

"Well, I'll give you two kids a moment together, but, Jena, your dinner is on the table, so don't take too long," Mr. Parker says.

Mrs. Parker peeks her head into the living room. "Jake, would you like to have some dinner?"

"Well, I am a little hungry," he says.

"Mom, could I have a few minutes with Jake?"

"Sure," Mrs. Parker replies.

Jena sits down next to Jake on the couch. "What are you doing out of the hospital? Did they release you, or did you just leave?" Jena asks.

Jake puts his hand on Jena's knee. "The doctor told my mom it was okay for me to go home, but I'm supposed to be in bed." Jake laughs. "I had to see you, Jena. I know you were a little shocked about my confession earlier today, so I had to know you were okay."

Jena looks down and then over at the house clock. Jake reaches over and gently lifts her face up to look at him. "Jena, I do love you. I really do," he says. "I love you as a friend, as a sister type, sort of ... and if one day, something more could happen, I'm sure I'll love you even more." Jake is silent for a second. "Our friendship means more to me than anything, and a part of being a friend is telling the truth." Jake gently touches Jena's face. "Now our friendship can truly grow." Jake tries to stand up. Jena helps him. "Well, I better be getting back home before my mom sends a squad car looking for me."

Mrs. Parker walks into the living room. "Jake, why don't you come in and have some hot food?"

Jena nods her head at Jake. Mrs. Parker insists. Jake takes a look at Jena. "All right," he replies. He takes his time walking into the kitchen. "Mrs. Parker, can I use the phone to call Mom to let her know where I am?"

"No worries, Jake. I've already talked to her. Now, have a seat." Mrs. Parker pulls a chair out for Jake.

Jena wraps her arms around Jake's and slowly helps him into the chair. Mr. Parker is sitting at the table picking at his food.

"So what's for dinner tonight?" Jake asks in an excited voice.

Mr. Parker stares up at Jake from his plate. "Huh, good question, Jake," he says in a sarcastic voice. "You have a right to know." He continues to poke fun. He leans close to Jake and tries to whisper, "Have you ever heard of a noloaf? Ever heard of that?" Mr. Parker smirks. Mrs. Parker gives him a quick glare. Jake shakes his head. "Well, son, it's the alternative to meatloaf, but don't let me spoil the fun."

Mrs. Parker hands Jake a plate, and he begins digging in. Jena, Mr. Parker, and Mrs. Parker stop and stare at Jake. Mrs. Parker turns and smiles at her husband. "You see, hon, someone likes my noloaf kind of cooking."

They all laugh. Jena reaches over to touch Jake's hand. "Slow down." Jake finishes his plate and licks the spoon. Mr. Parker just stares. "Mrs. Parker, this was one of the best meals I've had in a long time," he says. "I really mean it; this was great."

"Thanks, Jake." Mrs. Parker grins from ear to ear. Jena helps Jake get out of the chair. "Now you try to make it on home before your mom really sends out a squad car looking for you."

Jake kisses Mrs. Parker on the cheek. "Yes, ma'am." Jena walks Jake out to his car.

They both stop in front of his car. Jake turns toward her. "So we're good, right?" he asks. "I mean we're still best friends?"

Jena smiles at him. "Of course we're still best friends, jerk," she says. "What kind of stupid question is that?" She stops and stares at the McNeils' house. It only has one light on. There is a dark figure standing in the doorway staring back at her. It's Mr. McNeil. Jake turns around and sees Mr. McNeil standing in the doorway.

"Why is their house so dark?" he asks. "And why is Mr. McNeil standing in the doorway like some creeper?"

Jena stands closer to Jake. "I know, it's creepy, right? They were fighting earlier," she says.

"Who?" Jake asks.

"Them. The McNeils," Jena tries to speak quietly. "I also saw Mr. McNeil fighting with another woman at the hospital. I couldn't hear what they were saying, but she seemed pretty pissed at him. Then he came home, and Mrs. McNeil dug into him. The house has been dark for hours now," she says.

Jake looks back over, and Mr. McNeil is still standing in the dark doorway. "Now he's standing staring at us in his doorway like some crazy man. Maybe you guys should call the cops," Jake says. "I mean, who stands in a dark doorway for over five minutes? This guy has got to be nuts." Jake can see the fear in Jena's eyes. "Do you want me to say something to him, Jena?" Jake asks. "I mean if this creep is bothering you, I will go over there and kick his ass," he adds in a loud voice.

"Please stop." Jena puts her hand over Jake's mouth. "Look at you, you're barely getting around, and you want to kick someone's butt." Jena looks at Jake. "Okay, no more ass-kicking for you; it's time for you to go home and get to bed."

Jake gets into his car. "Yeah, you're right, but Jena ..." Jake tries to talk, but Jena is distracted.

"He's gone." Mr. McNeil is no longer standing in the doorway. The house is still dark, and there is no movement from Mrs. McNeil. Jena continues to be distracted by the darkness of the McNeils' house.

"Hey." Jake tries to get Jena's attention. "I'll see you at school tomorrow."

"Of course," Jena replies. "Wait, you're going to school?"

Jake sticks his hand out his car window. "Of course. Good night, banana head," Jake says as he backs out of the driveway. "And, oh, don't forget, you're still my prom date."

Jena shakes her head, smiles, and then walks toward her house. *I can't believe we're graduating in two weeks,* Jena thinks to herself. She opens the door. She hears a noise and turns around. Mr. McNeil is standing in the doorway with something in his hand. Jena rushes into the house and slams the door behind her.

CHAPTER THIRTEEN

Mr. and Mrs. Parker rush into the living room. "What in the hell is going on, Jena?" Mr. Parker yells. "Why did you slam the door?" he shouts as he opens the door.

Jena stands in a state of panic. She tries to speak, but fear has gotten the best of her. Mrs. Parker grabs Jena's arms. "Jena, speak to us. Is there something wrong with Jake?" Mrs. Parker asks. Mr. Parker rushes to open the front door to see if Jake is all right, but the car is gone. Mr. McNeil is still standing in his doorway, but Kitty doesn't notice him. The house is still dark, and Mrs. McNeil is nowhere to be found. "Jena, what is it?" Mrs. Parker continues to ask.

"It's Mr. McNeil; he just keeps on staring at me." Jena's hands start to sweat and shake. Mr. Parker stands next to Jena. "I saw him today." Jena says.

"Who?" Mr. Parker ask. "Miles?"

Jena nods her head yes. "I saw him arguing with another woman at the hospital."

Mrs. Parker folds her arms. "Is that why you rushed into the car?"

Jena sits down. "Yes, Mom." Jena has a terrified look on her face. "Mom, he seemed so mad at me," she says. "At first, he didn't see me, but when he was about to get into his car, he saw me on the bench, and then you drove up, Mom, and I hurried to get into the car."

Mr. Parker is furious and heads upstairs to his bedroom closet to grab his shotgun. He mumbles as he walks up the stairs. "God damn piece of shit gonna scare my daughter!" Mr. Parker rumbles upstairs searching for his gun and bullets. "If that asshole thinks he can terrorize my daughter, well, he's got to deal with me first."

Mrs. Parker runs up the stairs. "Now look, Jim, there's no need to get violent. I mean, he hasn't done anything."

Mr. Parker paces back and forth around the bedroom. "Oh yes he has, Kitty. Didn't you hear Jena downstairs? This asshole has been watching her like a creepy criminal standing in a dark doorway." Mr. Parker loads up his gun.

"We don't know that for sure."

Mr. Parker replies, "Are you calling our daughter a liar, Kitty?" he yells even louder. He pulls the window curtain back. He puts it back. "For all we know, Jane could be dead. I'm going over there to see what the hell is going on." Mr. Parker loads more bullets into his gun, quickly walks down the stairs, and heads out the front door to the McNeils'.

Jena and Mrs. Parker stare frantically out the living room window, and Jena turns to grab and hug her mother. "Mom, you've got to stop him!" Jena says.

Mrs. Parker opens the front door. "Jena, if you know anything about your father, there's one thing you can't do, and that is stop him from doing whatever the hell he wants to do."

Mr. Parker places the gun on his shoulder as he walks across the street. Mr. McNeil is standing still in his dark doorway. Mr. Parker walks up to Mr. McNeil. "What the hell is wrong with you, Miles? Why are trying to scare Jena?" He points the shotgun at Miles and tries to bully his way into the house. "And where in the hell is Jane?" he yells. Mr. McNeil just stands and stares at him. "What the hell is wrong with you, Miles? Are you deaf? I said, 'Where is Jane?'"

Mr. McNeil tries to take advantage of the darkness. He pulls Mr. Parker into the dark house. The two men begin to wrestle around the dark living room. Mr. McNeil reaches for a baseball bat he hides behind the door and starts swinging at Mr. Parker. Mr. Parker points his gun in the dark room and fires two times. "Miles, you don't want to do this. I'll shoot you. I'll shoot you dead. You want to mess with my baby girl." Mr. Parker trips over something in the dark. He falls and realizes it's a body. Mrs. McNeil's dead body lies under Mr. Parker. The gun falls out of his hands. He manages to get a grip on the gun. Mr. Parker is in shock as he feels Mrs. McNeil's blood-soaked dead body lying beneath him. He tries to get up but slips on her blood. "What the hell have you done, Miles?" Mr. McNeil manages to turn on the living room lamp. He stands with a bat in his hand and a blank face. His shadow flows over him like an overgrown giant. The bat rises. "Put it down, Miles!" Mr. Parker yells.

Mr. McNeil swings the bat at him, and Mr. Parker fires two shots; one hits Mr. McNeil in the arm and the other hits him in the leg. Mr. Parker manages to get up but slips again on Mrs. McNeil's blood. He stares down at Mrs. McNeil stiff body. She has been bleeding from the neck. He yells, "Kitty, Jena, call the police! Hurry! Call the police!" Mr. Parker tries to hold back his tears. He looks over at Mr. McNeil, who is bleeding heavily from his wounded arm and leg.

Mrs. Parker rushes into the house. She sees Mrs. McNeil's bloody body on the floor. "Oh my God! He killed her! You killed Jane!" she yells. She yells for Jena from inside the house. "Jena, call nine-one-one now!"

Jena picks up the telephone to dial 911. The operator answers. "Nine-one-one, how can I help you?"

"Help." Jena's voice seems weak at first.

"Ma'am, I need you to speak up. This is the nine-one-one operator, how may I help you?"

Jena screams, "You have to help us! He's crazy!"

"Ma'am, please calm down; we have your address. Is this where the problems is?"

"Next door."

"Ma'am?"

"Next door, she's dead."

"Who's dead, ma'am? Just hold on; we're sending a car," the operator assures her.

"Please hurry, my mother and father are next door, and they could be hurt. There's a crazy man next door. He's crazy, and I think he's going to kill my father."

"Okay, ma'am, we are sending a police car over right away. Please stay on the line and stay calm."

Jena stands in the doorway with the cordless phone. Mr. Parker keeps the gun held on Mr. McNeil. Mrs. Parker runs over to Jena. "Mom, they're coming!" Jena says.

"Okay, Jena, I'm going back over there," Mrs. Parker replies.

"No, Mom. Don't!" Jena pleads. "Please don't go back over there. I'm sure Dad is all right."

Mr. Parker leans over to see if Mrs. McNeil is still breathing. He puts down the gun and tries to perform CPR, but stops when he realizes she is dead. He turns to look at Mr. McNeil, who is still in the corner bleeding. "How could you kill your own wife?" Mr. Parker slips again in Mrs. McNeil's blood. The gun is flung out of his hand and over near the front door. Mr. McNeil reaches for the gun from the floor. He points it at Mr. Parker. "The same way I'm going to kill you and your damn nosey daughter," Mr. McNeil replies.

"You bastard!" Mr. Parker yells.

Mr. McNeil slowly aims the gun. Mr. Parker tries to get up, but his feet can't get traction on the wet floor. Mr. McNeil also struggles to get up. He finally manages to stand up, and he points the gun barrel down at Mr. Parker and fires twice. Mrs. Parker stands silently in the McNeils' doorway in shock at what she just saw. She is frozen in shock and horror. Mr. McNeil wobbles and holds the shotgun in his hand. Mrs. Parker stares as her husband lies with two gunshots to his head. Mrs. Parker screams and runs to him. "Honey, please don't die on me! Please," Mrs. Parker begs through her tears.

Mr. McNeil points the gun at Mrs. Parker and fires, but there're no bullets left. Mrs. Parker lies there holding Mr. Parker in her arms. Blood runs down her hands and arms. She uncontrollably cries, "No, please! Please don't take him, God!"

The police arrive. Kitty is holding her husband in her arms. She tries to shake him awake, but in a moment of silence, she realizes there is no hope. She pleads to God anyway, "Please don't take him."

Jena drops the telephone to the floor and rushes out the front door to the McNeils' house. Police squad cars are surrounding the McNeils' house. Mrs. Parker's grip on her husband is so strong that the police officer has to pry her hands loose. She pulls away from the officer with blood dripping from her hands and tears streaming down her face. She walks slowly to the McNeils' front yard and then falls to her knees. Jena walks outside, but she stops in the middle of the street. Mrs. Parker looks up at her with tears pouring down her face. Jena puts her hands over her eyes, hoping that when she removes them, this whole thing will have been just a nightmare. She stands still as if she were frozen in time. One look at her mother's face and she knows. She knows that her life will never be the same. She stands still in the middle of the street. Mrs. Parker cries hopelessly on her knees. She reaches for Jena to comfort her. Jena knows what horror lies in the house. It isn't something she can bear. It isn't something her reality can handle. She begins running, and tears stream down, falling behind her as the wind blows in her face. *How far should I run?* she wonders. *To the ends of the earth? To the sun and back? Or do I just stand here and let the pain disintegrate me until I'm dust or until I'm no more?* She keeps running and running until she reaches a dark neighborhood street. Out of breath,

Jena leans over coughing and breathing hard. She looks over at a house sign swinging from a fence. The sign reads "Beware of Dog." Jena tries to catch her breath, but she can't stop her thoughts of her mother's face and bloody hands. She begins to walk slowly down the dark street. The street is silent. No dogs are barking; no lights are on; and no people are walking or talking—just nothing. She continues to walk until she reaches Jake's house. Somehow, she can't remember how she got to Jake's house or how she knew where to find his house in the dark when she didn't even know where she was running to. Jake's house is dark, except for the TV in his room. He's asleep. Jena climbs up to Jake's bedroom window. She taps on the window very lightly. Jake doesn't move. Her hopelessness begins to set in again, but she knows he is the only person who can help her. She gives the window a harder tap. Jake wakes up and slowly walks toward his window. Jena is standing close to the window's edge. Jake opens the window, and Jena crawls in. Her eyes are red, full of tears.

Jake grabs her close to him. "Jena, what's wrong?" Jake whispers. Jena doesn't say a word. She just crawls into his bed. Jake doesn't ask her any more questions. He places his blanket over her body and watches while she falls asleep. Jake lies close to her, comforting her throughout the night. He places his arm around her body. He gently rubs her arm and then kisses her on the cheek. He whispers words of comfort to her. "Whatever it is, no matter what, I will be here for you." Jena lies motionless next to Jake. Her body is still chilled from the outside air. He keeps her close to him throughout the night. He stares at her, wishing he knew what or who had hurt her. Jake finally falls asleep from sheer exhaustion.

The morning sunlight shines through Jake's window and casts a shadow. Jena is standing in the window staring at the sunlight. Her body is exhausted from the night before. She turns around and realizes that Jake has just awakened. They stare at each other for a moment, and then Jena turns around to stare back at the brilliant sunlight.

CHAPTER FOURTEEN

Jake slowly removes the covers; the sunlight blinds him as he slides to the edge of the bed. Jena is still staring out the window. She doesn't move but stands still in front of the window slightly shadowing Jake. Jena speaks softly from the window. "Isn't the sun a beautiful thing, Jake?" she asks. "I mean, it rises without a sound, and then it disappears the same way." Jena speaks in a sad voice. "Without making sound. Yet we go on all day without noticing it sometimes. Without really appreciating how beautiful the sun, the moon, and the stars really are."

Jake stands up and walks toward Jena. "Jena, what's going on?" he asks. He touches her shoulder. "What's wrong?" Jena says nothing. She just stares at the sun. "You come to my room in the middle of the night upset and crying. I wanted to say something, but I didn't know what to say. All I know is that whatever it is, I want to be there for you." Jake moves closer to Jena.

Jena turns around and rushes into his arms. She begins to cry and presses her face into Jake's neck. Her tears fall down his neck to his shirt. "Jake, my father was killed last night by Mr. McNeil," Jena answers in a tearful voice.

Jake squeezes her body into his. He doesn't say anything at first. "What do you mean your father was killed last night?" he finally asks. "I just saw him at dinner." He is almost speechless.

Jena cries harder. Her body is limp, and hopelessness fills her world. Jake holds her tight and tries to comfort her. Jena releases Jake and walks to the bed to sit down. "I know, Jake, but that was then; now, he's gone. He's dead and my mother ..." Jena falls silent, trying hard to hold back more tears. "Oh God, the look on my mother's face when I saw her was too much for me to bear," Jena says. "So I ran. I ran before she could tell me what I already knew. I ran so I could be with you."

Jake kneels down next to her and lays his head on her knees. He then sits next to Jena on the bed. "So your mother doesn't know where you are right now?"

"No, she doesn't."

Jake reaches for her hand and places it in his. "Jena, you have to call her to let her know where you are and that you're all right," Jake says. "Ah damn, this is horrible." Jake stands up from the bed. "I can't believe what you're saying. Your dad is dead." Jake turns around. "What in the hell happened last night?" Jake asks.

Jena tries to wipe the tears from her eyes. She snuffles. "Mr. McNeil just flipped out. I saw him earlier yesterday at the hospital arguing with another woman. She seemed pretty pissed off at him. He knew I saw him, and I was scared. Then later that day, when Mom brought me home, I saw Mrs. McNeil on the phone arguing with someone. She seemed pissed too. I watched out of my window to find out what was going on, I lied to Mom. I lied and told her I didn't see anything ... but I did. I was staring from the living room window, and then I went upstairs to stare from my bedroom window." Jena looks up at Jake. "The house was dark and creepy. I saw Mr. McNeil come home, but when Mom asked me if I'd seen anything, I told her no. I just didn't want her to know that I'd been watching the McNeil house. I should have told her about what I saw at the hospital." Jena starts to cry again. "I should have told her that I saw him come home and that he was standing in the doorway in the dark just staring over at my house watching me and that this wasn't the first time. If I'd just said something, then maybe ..." Jena stops speaking and starts crying very hard. Jake tries to comfort her. "Jake, if I'd said something, maybe my dad would still be alive and maybe Mom would of have called the cops earlier. I was just too afraid to say anything. Now, my father's dead." Jake's door suddenly opens.

Mrs. Paterson stands in the doorway. "I've been listening to you two talk," she says. She walks over to give Jena a hug. She hugs her and starts to cry. "Your mother just called. I'm so sorry, Jena. I told her not to worry, because I just knew that you would be here with Jake. She has been trying to call all night, but I guess our phone was not working. I don't know. Please call your mother because she is extremely worried about you."

Jake says he'll get the phone from downstairs and bring it to Jena. "Jena, you need to call your mother now." Jake goes downstairs to get the living room cordless phone. Jena stands in his room with Mrs. Paterson, who has a terrified look on her face.

Jena notices that Jake is walking better. "He's doing a lot better, huh?"

Mrs. Paterson tries to speak, tries to talk through her tears. "Yes, he has been doing great since he left the hospital. Didn't you see him last night?" Mrs. Paterson asks.

Jena has a puzzled look on her face. She remembers Jake hardly being able to walk. Jake makes it back upstairs and hands Jena the telephone. She slowly takes the phone out of Jake's hand. "Come on, Jake, let's give Jena some privacy."

Jena dials her house number. Mrs. Parker answers the phone in a sad and sober voice. "Hello."

Jena is silent at first, and then she speaks. "Mom."

In a relieved voice, her mother says, "Jena, sweetie, I'm so happy to hear your voice."

"Mom." She tries not to cry. "Mom, I'm ..." Jena cries. "I'm sorry I ran away, but when I saw your face, I just couldn't ... I just couldn't bear to hear you say it. The look on your face made my heart drop, and all I could to do was run, run as fast as I could."

"I know, honey," Mrs. Parker says. "It's okay. I know that's why you ran." She sighs and then starts crying.

"Mom, I'm coming home."

"Jena, take as much time as you need. Right now, I don't know if I can hold an entire conversation without crying. I want you to come home, but I know you're grieving too. Let Jake comfort you."

"Mom, I need to be there to comfort you."

"Jena, come when you can ..." Mrs. Parker's voice fades into tears.

Jena can tell that her mother is no longer there with her but tries to talk her back to the conversation. "Mom, I'll be there soon." Mrs. Parker hangs up the phone. "Mom ... Mom!" Jena calls, but Mrs. Parker has already gone.

Jake walks back into the room. Jena sits on his bed without any words to say. She looks back up at the sun and then closes her eyes. Jake walks toward Jena, but she can't face him.

"Jena, I'll get dressed and take you home," Jake says.

"Thanks," she replies.

Jake takes his clothes out of the drawer and then leaves the room to get dressed. He returns to his room and finds Jena still sitting silently on the bed. "Are you ready?" Jake reaches his hand out to her.

"No, but let's go," she replies. Jena gets up from the bed. Jake puts his arms around her, and then they both walk out of the house to his car. They get into the car. Jake starts it up and backs out of the driveway. Trying not to look over at the McNeils', Jena stares straight ahead without moving. Jake pulls into her driveway. "I'm sorry that I got you out your of bed. I know you're not quite recovered," Jena says.

"Jena, I would do anything for you," Jake replies. "Anything." He gets out to open the car door for her. There are police officers still investigating the crime scene at the McNeils' house. Jena turns away from the McNeils' house as she gets out of the car. "Jena, I have something to say before you go into the house. I have to tell you that I heard on the news that Mr. McNeil is still alive," Jake explains.

"Your father shot him twice, but somehow, he managed to survive. I thought you'd rather hear this from me than from someone else," Jake continues to explain.

"Jake, isn't this supposed to be a good year? This is our senior year of high school. My best friend in the whole world just confessed that he's in love with me, my dad gets killed, and now I find out that the man who killed him lives? I don't know how I'm going to make it through this. I've always tried to do the right thing. Be a really … really good person." Jake grabs Jena's hand. "My dad always taught me to be the best person that I can be in this world, because he always said that there's enough evil and the world doesn't need any more. This is what he always taught me, and now look, his friend, our neighbor, was the very evil he was talking about. This evil lived right next door to us." Jena starts crying again. "Why couldn't he see that evil?" She looks over to Jake. "Huh? Why?" She walks to the front door. Jake calls to her, but she keeps on walking. She opens the door and then closes it behind her. Jake watches. He gets back into his car and drives away.

CHAPTER FIFTEEN

Jena walks into the house. It's quiet except for the cuckoo clock ticking. She gently closes the door behind her and then peeks out the living room window to watch as Jake drives away. Family photos are scattered throughout the house. Jena leans down to pick up a picture from the floor. "Dad," she quietly whispers. "Why?" She holds a picture in her hand of her dad teaching her how to play baseball when she was three years old. Jena stares at the photo and tears begin to flow from her eyes. She suddenly hears the rustling sounds of boxes, drawers, and closet doors opening and closing from upstairs. Mrs. Parker is mumbling as she scrambles to look for more pictures and anything her late husband had given her. Jena stands and stares at her mother as she rambles, throwing boxes and searching for photos and other mementos. "Mom!" Jena calls.

Mrs. Parker turns around for second to look at Jena, but she frantically continues to search for any pictures of her husband. Pretending like everything is fine, she says, "Oh, Jena, I'm glad you're home, because I need your help, dear." Jena looks around the disaster of a room. "We have to find all the pictures in the house that have Daddy in them." Mrs. Parker sounds a little crazy. "You see, we have to gather all these picture so we will never forget all the wonderful things he's done for this family." She paces around the room. "You know, all of our happy times—"

Jena interrupts her. "Mom, maybe you should just relax."

Mrs. Parker gives her an angry stare. "I can't relax right now," she replies. "I have too much to do," she says, sounding even more frantic. "I have to find these pictures, plan a funeral, and heck, your graduation is only weeks away." Mrs. Parker walks up to Jena. "You silly girl, I don't have time to relax." She lightly touches Jena's face. "You always make laugh. Ever since you were a little baby, you've made me laugh." Her voice cracks. Tears begin to run down her cheeks. "Jena, don't ever stop laughing in life." Jena hugs her mother. Mrs. Parker begins crying in Jena's arms. Speaking through her tears, she says, "Jena, please promise me you'll always laugh. Don't turn into a person who gives up on life." Trying to sound convincing, she says, "Jena, somehow or someway, we will get through this and we will go on."

Jena embraces her mother while she cries. Jena doesn't know what to say, so she just holds her mother close. "Mom, you're exhausted. You need to get some sleep." Jena sits her mother down. "We can look for the photos of Dad tomorrow, but today, you have to rest." She leans down toward her mother. "I know this is very rough for you, Mom, for the both of us, but like you said, somehow, we will get through this ... somehow, someway." Jena helps her mother lie down. She pushes the boxes of pictures, gifts, and other items her mom dug out to the other side of the bed. Mrs. Parker is exhausted and instantly falls asleep. Jena puts a blanket over her, kisses her on the forehead, and begins cleaning up her mom's room. She picks up a photo from off the floor. It's a photo of her dad when he was in the army. She kisses the photo and says, "Don't worry, justice will be served. One day, the sun will shine brighter than it's ever shone and that will be the day Mr. McNeil will pay."

Jena walks to her room. Her window is open, and there is a slight breeze blowing. Jena lies down on her bed and falls into a deep sleep. She begins to dream she's back on the airplane standing in the front row staring at all the faceless men.

Jena struts down the aisle waving a gun in her hand. Mr. McNeil is sitting in the back of the plane reading a newspaper. His face is visible to Jena. She points the gun at him. "What are you doing on this plane?" Jena asks.

Mr. McNeil puts the newspaper down. "Do I know you?" he asks.

"You must know me since you're on my airplane," she says.

Mr. McNeil looks around the airplane at the other passengers. Trying to talk tough, he says, "Look, lady, why don't you go and harass someone else. Can't you see I'm busy reading my paper?" Mr. McNeil raises his newspaper up so he can ignore Jena.

Jena pulls the top of the paper down with the gun. "So you don't remember, do you?" she says. Jena points the gun at Mr. McNeil's head. "Don't you know who you are?" she asks. "You're the evil that lives next door."

Jena fires the gun in her dreams. She suddenly wakes up and falls out of her bed to the floor. She places her hand over her face in disbelief. She walks to her mother's room to see if the abrupt fall woke her up. Mrs. Parker is still sound asleep. Jena begins cleaning up the house. She moves from room to room, cleaning the floors and walls, and she places the pictures back where they came from. She goes back upstairs to check on her mother. Mrs. Parker is still asleep. Jena takes a long shower and washes her face and hair. The steam from the shower fogs up the mirror in the bedroom. She wipes the steam away with her hands. She puts on fresh clothing, puts her robe over it, and slips into her night shoes. Then, she goes downstairs to start dinner. The doorbell rings, and she walks over and opens the door. Detective Martin is standing in the doorway.

"Sorry to visit your house so late, ma'am, but is Mrs. Parker available?" Detective Martin asks.

Jena closes her robe a little tighter. "My mother is asleep," she answers.

Looking in the house curiously, he says, "Well, okay, but when she wakes up, could you tell her that Detective Martin stopped by and I need her to answer a few more questions concerning the murder of her husband, your father."

Jena looks worried.

Detective Martin tries to comfort her. "I know this is a terrible time for you both, but the investigation must continue in order for us to bring your father's killer to justice."

Jena nods her head. "I understand, Officer," she replies. "I will tell my mother as soon as she awakes."

Detective Martin tips his hat. "Thank you, ma'am, and have a good night."

Jena closes the front door. She walks back into the kitchen and opens the cabinet door. Cans of sweet peas are lined up perfectly and take up most of the space on one of the shelves. Jena reaches for one of the cans. She holds the can tightly in her hands. "Dad's favorite … sweet peas," Jena says with a smile.

Mrs. Parker awakes. She calls for Jena. Jena closes the kitchen cabinet door and puts the can of sweet peas on the counter. "Coming, Mom!" she yells. She walks through the living room, up the stairs, and then to her mother's room.

Mrs. Parker is lying in the bed turned sideways toward the room's door. Jena stands in the doorway. Her mother waves for her to come closer. "I see someone took a shower." She smiles.

Jena moves closer to her mom. "Yes, I thought it was time I stopped torturing my nostrils," Jena says with a smirk.

"What were you doing downstairs?" Mrs. Parker asks.

Jena sits on the bed. "Well, I was attempting to make dinner," she replies.

"Dinner? You?" Mrs. Parker says in a sarcastic voice.

"Uh, yeah, Mom, I think I can manage making something for dinner for us," Jena replies.

"Okay then, the kitchen is yours."

Jena stands up and starts to head back downstairs. She turns around quickly. "Oh, Mom, there was a police officer who came by; it was Detective Martin. He came by to speak to you, but I told him you were asleep."

Mrs. Parker remains silent for moment. She removes the covers and jumps out of bed. She looks over to Jena, "Well, just as well. I'm really not in the mood to talk to anyone except you, Jena." She touches Jena's face. "I have his card; I'll give him a call tomorrow."

Jena can see the sadness and disappointment on her mother's face. She listens as her mother begins to mumble words to herself as if she were talking to her dad. Mrs. Parker walks out of the bedroom and passes Jena without saying a word to her. Jena knows her mother is very upset by the death of her father, but there is also something strange about her, something different. Jena knows her mother isn't the same person she was yesterday or even the person she will be tomorrow.

CHAPTER SIXTEEN

Jena walks down the stairs holding her head low, thinking about her dad and the wonderful times they'd had when she was little. She walks into the kitchen, pulls out a pot from the bottom shelf, and then grabs two cans of sweet peas from the kitchen cabinet. *Yeah, that's what we'll have tonight, Dad's favorite, sweet peas,* Jena thinks to herself. *We'll have Dad's favorite, and I bet I'll make Mom smile.* Jena starts to hum while making dinner.

Mrs. Parker walks into the kitchen. "Ah, I know that smell." She sounds excited.

Jena and her mother sit down to dinner and talk for hours. Jena tells stories about her father from when she was a kid. They laugh, cry, and then laugh again throughout the night. "Jena, you know your dad loved you so much," Mrs. Parker says. "He really wanted the best for you, and so do I. I know he would want you to graduate high school and then to go straight to college." Mrs. Parker grabs Jena's hand. "I want you to go to college." She puts her head down and then raises it up again. "We've been saving for college since you were born. Your dad worked day and night for us to have a good life and for you to go to college." She looks away with uncertainty on her face. "We will get through this terrible time, but when it's all over, you can't stay here with me; you have to go to college," she insists. "You have to go on with your life. I will be right here whenever you need me, honey."

Jena walks over to give her mother a great big hug. She puts her forehead against her mother's and then kisses it. "Thank you, Mom," Jena says tearfully. "Thank you."

Jena and her mother spend the entire week planning her father's funeral. Family, friends, and co-workers of Mr. Parker stop by the house to offer their condolences. The funeral takes place on a Saturday. Jena and her mother both cry tears of disbelief. Mr. Parker's longtime friend and his sister eulogized him. Jena fell to her knees when they opened her dad's casket. Mrs. Parker fainted and had to be carried out of the church. Jena reaches for her mother's hand as they carry her out of the church, but her mother is totally withdrawn from sheer sadness. At the grave site, Jena and her mother hold hands as the pallbearers lower her father into the ground. Autumn leaves blow through the mid-evening air. Mr. Parker's sister Denise reaches for Mrs. Parker to walk her away from the grave. Jena refuses to leave. Jake stands next to her. There is a silence at first, and then Jena speaks.

"Sorry, I haven't spoken to you in a week, but I've been trying to spend time with my mother. She has been trying to pretend that she is all right, but as you can see, she has fallen completely apart. I know a large part of my mother died with my dad." Jena turns to look at Jake. "Some people can go on, I suppose, but I think my mother might not be able to withstand the loneliness," she says. She looks up at the sky.

Jake turns Jena around to face him again, stares her deeply in the eyes, and then squeezes her close to him. "I'll do whatever it takes to make sure you're happy again," Jake whispers in her ear. "Whatever it takes. Jena, you mean the entire world to me." He kisses her gently on the cheek.

Jena takes one last look at her father's grave site. "Let's go, Jake." She reaches for his hand. They both walk away from the grave site to his car and then drive away. Jake turns on the radio in his car. The radio news broadcasts an all points bulletin that a man alleged to be the murderer in the killing of Mr. Jim A. Parker, Mr. Miles McNeil, has escaped from St. Mary's Hospital. Jena turns the radio up. The radio announcer continues to speak. "Police officers are asking that everyone keep their doors locked and eyes out for this man. If you see him, please contact the Maple County Sheriff's Department." Jena turns off the radio. Jake puts his foot on the gas. He pulls up to Jena's house.

Police officers are surrounding the house. Jena opens the car door and begins to get out. "Jena, wait." Jake leans out the car window. "Jena, I want to come inside even if it's just for a little while just to make sure you and your mother are all right."

"All right, but I'm not afraid of Mr. McNeil," Jena replies.

"I know, but I'd like to come in just the same," Jake pleads. Jake and Jena walk into the house. Mrs. Parker is sitting on the couch watching the news.

The news is reporting the escape. Jena walks over to turn the TV off. "I guess you already heard?" Mrs. Parker says.

"Yes, Mom, but we're not going to let that maniac run our lives." Jena turns around to look at Jake. "We aren't going to let this control our lives."

Mrs. Parker gets up from off the couch and walks upstairs. Jena turns to Jake. "Jake, I'm not afraid of him, and I'm not letting him control our lives," she repeats. Jena walks into the kitchen and grabs two waters out of the refrigerator. She sits down on the couch. Jake sits next to her. "Here." Jena pushes a water bottle toward Jake. "I'd offer you something stronger, but neither of my parents drink," Jena says.

Jake plays with the water bottle for a moment. Surprised at how Jena is acting, he says, "Water is fine."

Jena stands up. "Jake, I'm coming to school tomorrow."

Sounding surprised, he replies, "Okay."

"We are graduating soon, and I plan on walking down the aisle to get my diploma," she says. "I've earned it, and my father would be proud of me." In an angry voice, Jena continues, "And neither Mr. McNeil nor anything else is going to stop me from being the person that my father wanted me to be." Jena opens her water bottle and then takes a sip. She leans over.

"Jena, are you all right?" Jake asks.

"I'm fine, Jake," Jena answers softly. "I'm just fine." She gets up from the couch. "Look, thank you for bring me home and for being here for me. You are an incredible friend." She walks toward the front door signaling that it's time for Jake to leave. Jake places the water bottle on the living room table and then walks toward the door. Jena opens the front door. The police officers are outside laughing and smoking cigarettes. Jena gives them a mean look. Jake starts to walk out. On impulse, Jena grabs him and kisses him fiercely on the lips. "See you tomorrow."

Jake is surprised. He licks his lips and then shakes his head. "Yeah. See you tomorrow," he replies. Jena closes and locks the door, grins a little, and then turns off the downstairs lights and walks upstairs.

CHAPTER SEVENTEEN

Jena passes her mother's room. Her door is slightly ajar, and she can see her kneeling down praying. Jena quickly walks away to her own room. She lies down on her bed and falls into a deep sleep. Jena awakes suddenly the next day.

Mrs. Parker is standing over her bed. Startled by her mom's presence, Jena asks, "Mom, what are you doing here?"

"Jena, I was thinking that maybe I should sell the house and move somewhere up north, near Grandma."

Jena moves closer to the edge of her bed. "Mom, I'm still here with you. I mean, I haven't gone to college yet. And besides, you and Grandma don't really get along too well."

Mrs. Parker shakes her head. "Yeah, you're right," she replies. "But maybe it's time that I try to make things right with her. Maybe I should try before something else happens." Mrs. Parker walks out of Jena's room. She gently closes the door behind her.

Jena gets out of bed and stands in front of her mirror. She looks deeply into the mirror at herself. "Who are you?" she asks herself.

Mrs. Parker rushes back to Jena's room and opens the door.

"Mom, what's wrong? You scared me." Jena says.

Mrs. Parker's strange behavior is starting to worry Jena. "Sorry, honey," Mrs. Parker replies. "I just wanted to tell you not to be late for school."

Jena stands in front of the mirror feeling uneasy about her mom's sudden burst of energy. Jena hesitates to reply. "I won't be late, Mom."

Mrs. Parker slams the door. Jena walks away from the mirror, takes a shower, and then gets ready for school. She slowly walks down the stairs.

Mrs. Parker is humming in the kitchen while cooking breakfast. Jena slowly opens the door and then sneaks out. She stops outside to stare at the McNeils' house, and then she continues to walk to school.

A car pulls up behind her and honks its horn. Jena turns around. Jake sticks his head out the window. "Want a ride, pretty lady?"

Jena turns around and then smiles. "Maybe," she replies. She stands near the car door.

"Okay then, girl, let's go," Jake says.

Jena gets into the car. Jake turns up the radio and then drives off. Jena turns the radio down. "Jake, I think my mother is having a nervous breakdown," she says.

"Why? What's up?" he asks.

"Well, she's just acting strange. I mean she popped into my room and scared the living hell out of me," Jena says. "I know that popping into someone's room isn't enough to call nine-one-one or anything like that, but it's just the way she did it. It's like she's not herself. Do you know what I mean?" Jena asks.

"Yeah, I guess, Jena," Jake replies. "I'm sure your mom is just going to through some changes. She'll come around to being her old self." Jake pulls into the school's student parking lot. "Jena, she just lost her husband, so maybe she's just trying to pull herself back together," Jake adds.

Carol, Chance, and Ken are all standing in the parking lot talking. Jake pulls into a parking space. "So it looks like everyone got released from the hospital at the same time," Jena says sarcastically.

Jake turns off the car engine and then glances over at Ken. "I guess so."

Jake and Jena get out of the car.

"Hey, Jena!" Chance calls. "Hey, Jena, come over here!"

Jena yanks on Jake's coat. "Come on, you."

Jena and Jake walk over to Chance. "So, look." Chance wraps her arms around Ken.

Carol gives Jena a big hug. "Jena, I'm so sorry about your dad," she says.

"Yeah, Jena, that was bullshit what Mr. McNeil did, and now he's running around free somewhere." Ken says.

Jena looks down at the ground. "Hey, guys, can we change the subject?" Jake says.

Chance jumps up from where she is sitting on Ken's car. "Well, I see we all made it out of the hospital." She laughs. Carol puts her arms around

Ken. Chance reaches to take Carol's arms off and puts her arms around Ken instead. "Yeah." Looking over at Carol, she says, "And we're all out just in time to graduate from high school. Isn't that great?" She kisses Ken on the lips.

Carol backs away with a frown on her face. "So, Jena, what're your plans after high school?" she asks.

Jena glances over at Jake. "I plan on going to college," she replies.

"Hey, me too!" Chance says. "Ken and I got accepted at Northwest University."

"Wow, that's great, so did I!" Jena replies in an excited voice.

Carol stares at Chance and Ken with a disappointed look on her face. "Jake, where did you get accepted?" she asks.

Jake looks away, trying to avoid the question.

"Well?" Carol asks again.

"Just about every college I applied too," he replies in smart voice. "What about you, Carol?" he asks.

Carol kicks her foot around. "Well, I don't have any acceptance letters yet, but there's still time, right, guys?" Carol answers in a skeptical voice.

Jena turns to Jake. "Well, we have to go," she says. "I can't be late for class."

Chance nudges Ken to say something. Jake and Jena begin walking away. "Hey, you guys?" Ken calls. Jena and Jake turn around. "I'm having a graduation party next week. I know we've had our differences, but you are welcome to come."

Jake walks back to Ken. "Thanks, man." He reaches out to Ken. They shake. Jake turns around, and he and Jena walk to class.

"Huh." Jena begins to speak.

"Jena, don't say anything," Jake replies.

"Okay, I won't." She smiles. Jake walks Jena to her class, kisses her on the cheek, and then rushes off to his class. "See you second period!" Jake yells as he races down the hallway.

Not looking where he is going, he accidently bumps into Principal Ricky. "Slow down, kid," Principal Ricky says. Jena walks into her class and closes the door.

Ms. Pickens walks up to Jena before she sits down. "Jena, sweetie, I'm so sorry about what happened to your father," she says. "If there's anything I can do or if you're having difficulty concentrating on class, please let me know. The school does understand that you're in the grieving process." She touches Jena's shoulder.

"Thanks, Ms. Pickens, but I'll be fine," Jena replies. She sits down at her desk.

The national anthem comes over the intercom, and afterward, Principal Ricky makes an announcement. "To our high school seniors, you will be graduating in just two weeks. Make sure you do your best to maintain the fine quality of statesmanship you have demonstrated throughout the year. Certainly, our school has its ups and downs like any other school, but at Maple Landing High, we are fighting, and we don't quit," Principal Ricky continues. 'No!" he screams into the intercom. "No, we keep going. So, seniors and the rest of the school, keep going. Thanks to you all! This is a message from your principal. Have a great day!"

The entire class starts laughing out loud. "I think Principal Ricky is a freak," one student says.

"No, he's just straight-out crazy," another student replies.

"I think I'm going to puke!" another student yells out.

"Okay, class, settle down, and let's get started for the day," Mrs. Pickens says.

Jena sits at her desk thinking about her mother, graduation, and Jake, the three most solid things she has in life.

The student sitting behind Jena leans over in his chair and whispers in her ear, "If I was you, Jena, I'd track down Mr. McNeil and kill him."

Ms. Pickens walks around the class with a stack of papers in her hand. "All right, everyone, it's pop quiz time."

"Aww, man!" echoes throughout the classroom.

Jena stares off into the classroom. Ms. Pickens hands Jena her test and leans over to whisper in her ear. "Don't worry, Jena, if you have difficulty, just let me know."

Jena nods her head. Ms. Pickens puts the test facedown on her desk and then continues handing the test out to the rest of the class.

CHAPTER EIGHTEEN

Jena completes her test within fifteen minutes. She spends the rest of time thinking about her father and mother. She thinks back to the night her father died and the devastated look on her mother's face after McNeil shot him in cold blood, how she ran and ran until she couldn't run anymore, and the pain and the total mental exhaustion she felt as a daughter who'd lost one of the greatest dads in the world.

Principal Ricky enters the classroom just before the school bell rings. He speaks to Ms. Pickens privately, and then Ms. Pickens calls Jena over to them. "Jena, Principal Ricky would like for you to see him in his office."

She feels immediate concern for her mother. "Is there something wrong?" Jena asks.

"We'll talk about it in my office," Principal Ricky replies.

Jena follows Principal Ricky to his office. He walks swiftly, leaving Jena a little behind. He tries to make Jena feel comfortable. He turns to look at her before opening his office door. Touching Jena on the shoulder, he says, "The office tried to call Ms. Pickens' room, but the phone apparently isn't working." Principal Ricky allows Jena to walk into his office first.

Officer Reyes is standing near a corner in the office. "Come in, Jena, and have a seat," he says. Principal Ricky closes his door behind him. He sits down in his chair. Officer Reyes sits in the chair next to Jena. He gives her a concerned look. "First, Jena, I want to say I'm very sorry about your father." Jena looks away, as if she's fed up with hearing people say they're sorry.

"I know you and your father were very close. I grew up with John, so I understand your pain. This is a sad time for all of us, dear," Principal Ricky says.

Officer Reyes faces Jena. "Jena, someone has reported seeing Mr. McNeil in this area."

Jena stands up. "But my mom—"

Before Jena can finish, Officer Reyes speaks. "Jena, please have a seat."

Jena sits back down. "We're keeping a close watch on your house and you. That's why I asked Principal Ricky to call you to the office. If you see Mr. McNeil or if he contacts you, please call the police right away. Again, your mother is fine. We have a car at the house and a police officer checks on her every hour. We will be here for the both of you and this community for as long as it takes to get this killer."

"Jena, I'm recommending that you be released from school early today," Principal Ricky says. "Officer Reyes will escort you home."

Jena stands up and throws her book bag over her shoulder. Officer Reyes opens the door. Jena begins to walk out and then stops. She turns around and stares at the two men. "I'm not going to let Mr. McNeil or anyone make me live my life in fear," she says. "He's already taken my father, and I'm not going to let him control my life too." Jena walks quickly and fiercely to Officer Reyes's car. She gets in the car and slams the door.

Officer Reyes stares back at Jena in the rearview mirror. "Are you all right, young lady?" he asks.

Jena ignores him and stares off out the window. Officer Reyes continues to drive Jena home. He pulls into the driveway. There are two officers sitting in the police car in front of the house. Jena quickly gets out and walks into the house without saying a word. When she enters the house, she finds Mrs. Parker asleep on the living room couch. Jena tries to walk softly up the stairs, but a creak from one of the broken stairs wakes her mother.

"Jena?" Mrs. Parker calls.

Jena stops. "Yes, Mom?" She kneels near her mom on the couch. "Mom, just go back to sleep," she whispers. "I know everything, and I don't want you to worry about me." Mrs. Parker doesn't reply. She drifts back to sleep. Jena walks around the living room. She tries to be quiet, but Mrs. Parker wakes again.

"Jena?"

"Mom, I'm here," she says quietly.

Mrs. Parker falls back to sleep again. Jena walks upstairs. She falls asleep on her bed. In the morning, she gets up and finds Mrs. Parker still asleep on the couch.

At school, Jake approaches her at her locker. "Hey, you," he says.

"Hi," Jena says in a sad voice.

"Crazy times, huh?" Jake asks.

"Yeah, crazy times."

Jake tries to cheer Jena up. "Well, at least we have prom in two days," he says.

"We?" Jena acts surprised.

"You know 'we,' as in me and you?" Jakes jokes.

Jena closes her locker door. "Of course, silly."

Jake tries to hold back his excitement and quickly changes the subject. "So are you going to Ken's party tonight?" he asks. "I'm thinking about going."

"I don't think that would be a good idea, Jake." Jena stands still for a moment. "I mean you and Ken just had a fight that landed the both of you in the hospital."

"Yeah, I know." Jake reaches for Jena's books.

"What are you doing?" Jena is surprised.

"I'm being a gentleman."

Jena walks closer to Jake. "Jake, I can carry my own books," she replies. "You know, maybe going to the party would be a good idea, because then maybe you guys could find a way to move past this. You know … act like adults."

"Yeah, maybe we should go," Jake says in a hesitant voice.

"Well, I'll be there, so if you want to see me, then you'll be there," Jena teases Jake, gives him a flirtatious smile, and then walks away.

Carol stops Jena on her way to class. "Going to the party tonight, Jena?"

Jena nods her head and keeps walking. Carol walks next to her. "Well, that's good news," Carol says.

"Yeah, sure, why not?" Jena replies.

Carol walks with Jena to her class. "Jena, I'm going to tell Chance how I feel about Ken tonight." Jena stops. "I really feel it's time I stop pretending that I don't love Ken." Carol gently touches Jena's shoulder and then walks to class. Jena stands in the hallway with a shocked look on her face.

In homeroom, Chance sits in the desk next to Jena's. "Hi, Jena."

Jena sits down. "Hi."

"So, Ken's party is tonight. I hope you and Jake will be there."

Jena hesitates a little. "I'll be there. I don't know about Jake."

"I understand," Chance says. "Jake may need a little more time to get over things."

The homeroom teacher walks in, and Chance and Jena don't speak to each other again until after class. Chance gathers her things and catches up with Jena before she leaves. "Jena, why don't you come to my house to get ready for the party? I have a closet full of clothes, so I'm sure you'll find something. Carol will be there too."

Jena swallows. Feeling sorry for Chance, she says, "Oh, okay, sure, why not?"

The school day goes along as usual. In every class, Jena is bored and can't wait for the end of the day. Carol and Chance are waiting for Jena after school. The three girls head to Chance's house. They try on clothes and makeup. Jena watches while Chance giggles and jokes with Carol. Chance's mother calls for her from downstairs.

"Coming, Mom!" Chance yells back. "Gotta go see what Mom wants. I'll be back." Chance admires one of her dresses on Jena. "Jena, you look great." Chance leaves the room.

Jena tries to talk Carol out of telling Chance the truth. "Carol, are you sure you want to reveal your love for Ken tonight?" Jena asks.

Without blinking an eye, she says, "Yes." Carol continues to try on Chance's dresses.

"But you and Chance are best friends," Jena says. "How could you do something like that?"

Carol just stares at Jena. She throws Chance's dress on the floor. "Yes, we are friends, Jena, but I love Ken and I want to be with him. Don't you think that Chance deserves the truth? Haven't you ever been in love before? Don't you love Jake?"

Before Jena can reply, Chance returns to the room. "So, girls, have we found the perfect dress? We've got to show our asses off tonight." Chance has huge smile on her face. Jena looks at Carol with a disappointed expression on her face. All she can think is, *How can a person be so cruel by pretending to be a best friend when she is just a straight backstabber?* The girls continue to get dressed, but Jena is uneasy about Carol's true intentions. Jena wants to tell Chance the truth about Carol's motives, but she just can't. She watches as Carol continues to carry on as if she were a real friend to Chance. *If only Chance knew how evil Carol is, I know she would get her revenge,* she thought.

CHAPTER NINETEEN

The girls leave Chance's house to head to Ken's party. They pull up to the house. Ken is standing outside with two other guys smoking a cigarette. Chance pretends to run Ken over with her car. "You better get out of my way or suffer my hot wheels on your hot ass!" she yells out the car window with a smile, and then she bursts into laughter. Carol turns to her and gives her a mean look. Ken walks up to the car. He peeks in the backseat and smiles at Jena.

"Hi, Jena," he says. Noticing Jena has one of Chance's dresses on, he adds, "Hot dress." Ken's eyes are glued on Jena.

"Thanks, Ken," she replies.

Chance waves her hand in Ken's face. "Hey, lover, I'm the only girl you're supposed to be admiring," she says jealously.

Trying to get noticed, Carol says, "Hi, Ken," with a big, bright smile.

Not even looking at her, he ignores her and kisses Chance on the lips. Ken opens the driver door for Chance. "Let's go, baby. It's time to party." They all rush to get into Ken's house where the party is jumping. Jake is across the street watching them from behind a tree. He stands in the dark where no one can see him. The DJ in Ken's house is rocking the music. Jena walks to the kitchen where it's quiet. Ken follows her.

"So, Jena …" He circles her. "What's going on?" Ken moves closer to her.

Trying to ignore him, she says, "Not much, Ken. I'm just chillin', waiting to graduate just like you."

Carol stands behind the kitchen door to eavesdrop on their conversation.

"Jena, I know you don't think I like you, but it's really the opposite."

Carol opens her mouth wide. Ken smirks a little. He leans closer to Jena. "Why do you think I don't like Jake? Hmm?" Ken asks. "I don't like Jake because he's always been able to get close to you when I couldn't." Ken moves closer.

Jena steps back from Ken. "Ken, I think you've had a little too much to drink," Jena replies.

He grabs Jena's arm. "No, Jena." Ken leans in to kiss her. She moves back from him. "I'm just being honest," he replies. "I like you." Ken moves even closer to her. "I like you a lot."

"What about Chance, Ken?" Jena says in a dismissive voice. "How do you think she'll feel about your feelings toward me?" Jena tries to walk away.

Ken grabs her arm again. "Chance and I are just a high school fling." He pushes Jena up against the kitchen counter.

Carol bursts into the kitchen. "Ken, what are you talking about?" she yells in pissed-off voice. The music stops. Chance and a group of people rush into the kitchen. "What do you mean you like her?" Carol points to Jena. Carol pushes Jena out of the way. "Ken, I've loved you for all this time and watched while you cuddled up to Chance, and now you like Jena?" Carol says in a nasty tone.

Chance walks further into the kitchen. "What's going on here, guys?" Chance pushes Ken. A crowd of people pile up in the kitchen doorway. "What's going on in here?" Chance repeats.

Carol walks up to Chance, gets in her face, and points at her. "I'll tell you what's going on. I'm in love with Ken, and he likes Jena while at the same time, he's dating you."

Chance moves closer to Carol. She pushes her. Carol pushes her back. The two girls begin to fight. They tussle on the floor, and Ken and Jena try to break them up. Ken pulls Carol off of Chance. Carol punches Ken in the face, gives Jena a dirty look, and then runs out of the kitchen, crying, shoving, and telling them to get out of her way. Chance sits on the floor with a busted lip and black eye. Her hair is tangled, and her clothes are torn. Ken reaches to help her up, but Chance slaps his hand away. She stands up and slowly walks out of the kitchen through the crowd.

Jena walks up behind her. "Chance, wait!" she calls.

Chance turns to look at Jena. "Don't say anything to me."

"Chance, it's not my fault!" Jena yells.

Chance walks out of Ken's house, gets into her car, and slams the door. She drives off in a rage. Jake steps out from the shadow of the tree. He tries to stop Chance, but she just keeps on driving. Jena walks outside with Ken. A crowd of people from school follow them. Jake stands in the middle of the street wondering what happened.

Carol comes from out of nowhere. "Jake, you should kick Ken's ass," she says angrily. "He just admitted that he's in love with Jena."

Ken has an angry look on his face. "I never said I was in love with Jena!" he yells. "I just said I liked her."

Carol just gives him a mean look.

"And what's wrong with that?"

Jake is pissed off. "Oh, dude, you really are a piece of work."

Jena stands in between the two boys. "Look, there's not going to be any more fighting tonight." She pushes the two boys back. "Everyone, just calm down." She reaches her hand out to Jake. "Jake, let's go."

Jake doesn't move an inch. Jena tugs on his coat. Jake and Ken stand and stare each other down. "Jake, let's go," Jena says again as she pulls harder on his coat.

Jena starts walking, and Jake follows. They begin walking down the dark street quickly. "I thought you said you weren't coming, Jake," she says.

"I wasn't there," he answers. "I wasn't there. I was hiding behind a tree."

"Hiding?" Jena yells.

"I was waiting outside for you, but it looks like all the action was going on inside the house." Jake stops. "What's going on, Jena?"

Jena stops walking.

"Why is Carol so mad?"

Jena is hesitant to answer. She puts her hand on her hips. "Well, Carol overheard Ken saying that he likes me, and then Carol and Chance got into a fight." Jena raises her hand in the air. "Carol has had a secret crush on Ken. So does this sound like a soap opera to you?" Jena asks.

"No, it sounds like I should've kicked Ken's ass."

Jena leans over as if she feels sick. "Carol was going to confess her love tonight, but Ken crushed her heart when she overheard him telling me he likes me." Jena runs her hand through her hair.

"What a jerk," Jake says. "You know I've never liked him, and now I know why. How can you be friends with someone that you just want to beat the crap out of every single day?" Jena sits on the street curb. "I guess now we know what prom's going to be like."Jake sits next to her. "Hey, you want to blow off prom and just go to dinner or just hang somewhere else?" he asks.

"You know, after tonight, that actually doesn't sound too bad," Jena says. "At this point, I don't think that prom is going to be much fun." Jena kicks a piece of paper lying on the ground. Sighing, she says, "Jake, we can't just miss prom. It's our senior prom. Why don't we just walk in and walk back out?" Jena glances at him. "Just to say that we went." She shrugs her shoulders. "Just a suggestion."

Jake stands up. "Well, we better head back to Ken's house," he says.

"Why?" Jena asks.

"Because that's where my car is parked," Jake replies in joking voice. "Did you think we were walking to your house?"

Jena and Jake both start laughing. She shoves Jake a little. Jake stops to lean over to hug her, but she turns away. "Hey, remember when you stole my lunch and tried to blame it on poor Steve?"

Jake laughs.

"Oh come on, you know I didn't do it."

"What I know, Jake, is that you had peanut butter all over your hands and shirt and your mom didn't make you that for lunch." Jena smiles. "I was so mad at you."

Jake puts his arm around Jena. They begin walking back to his car. No words are spoken. Jena glances over at Jake just to see the expression on his face. He is smiling, and for a moment, Jena feels like she is in love with him. Jake leans over and kisses her on the forehead.

"You're the bestest friend a guy could have," he says.

Jena smiles. "You too," she says.

He stares at her. They finally get to Jake's car, and he drives her home.

CHAPTER TWENTY

On the phone, Jena asks, "Okay, so you're wearing what?"

"I have on a duck suit, carrot-head wig, Charlie Chapman hat, and I'm wearing a weird beard."

"Ah ... yeah, that sounds crazy, Jake."

"And you?" he asks.

Jena looks in the mirror. "Well, I'm ... dressed like a clown."

Jake laughs uncontrollably. "A clown? Come on, you couldn't have been something a little sexier?"

"Look, you said we're just going to walk in and walk out, so what does it matter what I wear?" Jena's doorbell rings. "Hold on, Jake, someone's at the door."

Jena opens the door, and it's Jake standing in the doorway. "Oh, that's unique," she says.

"Ha! You fell for it," he replies.

They both stare each other and laugh. Jena peeks out into the driveway. "Let's get out of here before my mom catches me and makes me take this clown suit off. I told her we were skipping the prom and going to your house to watch movies because what school has prom right before graduation?"

He says, "Hurry up," and closes the door. He stops and stares at Jena before she gets into the car. "You know you still look good even in that clown suit."

Surprised, she smiles. "You think so?"

"No, I was just being nice; you're a clown for goodness' sake." Jake chuckles.

"Oh, but a carrot-head wig is something to brag about?" Jena says. In the car, they both poke fun at each other.

"Clown."

"Carrot Head."

CHAPTER TWENTY-ONE

Two weeks pass, and it's only one day away from graduation. "Wanted" posters of Mr. McNeil are plastered all over the neighborhood and surrounding areas. Police officers continue to keep a watchful eye on Jena's house, while still searching for clues to where Mr. McNeil could be hiding. Mrs. Parker has not said a word for two weeks. She sits in front of the window daily just staring out. Jena hasn't spoken to Chance, Carol, or Ken since the night of the party. The day of graduation is joyful yet gloomy for Jena. Jena helps her mother get dressed for the graduation ceremony.

Jena hasn't spoken to any of her friends other than Jake about her father's murder by a man who still can't be found. She stands in front of her room mirror adjusting her cap and gown. She removes a picture of her parents from her mirror. The smiles on her mother's and father's faces make her feel sad. She remembers how happy her parents were back then. She thinks back to the many nights she sat on the stairway out of sight and watched while they cuddled and danced quietly. How her dad had held her mother in his arms and the gentle kisses he gave her on her cheeks while they danced to their favorite song. "If I Can't Have You, I Don't Want Nobody, Baby" by Yvonne Elliman. Jena remembers thinking at the time that her parents were the happiest people on earth and that she hoped to one day find a love like theirs. Jena puts the picture back on her mirror. She walks to her mother's room, but she isn't there.

"Mom!" Jena calls.

Jena walks downstairs, and Mrs. Parker is standing by the door holding her keys in her hands. Jena tries to take the keys from her mother's hand.

Mrs. Parker grips the keys tightly. "Mom, you can't drive," Jena says. "Jake's mother is going to pick us up. They will be here in a few minutes. Just have a seat until they get here."

Mrs. Parker lets go of the keys. Jena puts the keys down on the living room table. She peeks out the living room window. Jake's mother is just pulling up in the driveway. She reaches over to give her mother a hand. "It's time to go, Mom."

Mrs. Parker stands up and gently touches Jena's face. She has a proud, but sad look on her face. Jena knows what she is thinking, even if she doesn't say a word. Jake rings the doorbell, and Jena opens the door. She grabs her mother's purse on the way out the door. The graduation ceremony is crowded. There are students, parents, and proud grandparents everywhere. Mrs. Paterson takes Mrs. Parker to the seating area. Jena and Jake take their chairs for the ceremony. Chance, Ken, and Carol all pass them by, but no one says a word. Everyone seems eager for the ceremony to be over, but Jena cherishes the moment. This is the moment her dad talked about for months before he died: the moment that she would reach for her diploma when the principal called out the name "Jena Parker," she whispered quietly to herself.

"Jena Parker!" Principal Ricky calls.

Jena realizes she is being called. Time must have passed her by as she daydreamed. This is the moment, the moment Jena's been waiting for. Jena stands tall and walks up to get her diploma. People in the audience are standing up cheering and clapping for her. Jake jumps out of his seat and cheers the loudest.

Jena looks out into the crowd to find her mother. Mrs. Parker is standing with one arm up in the air trying to wave at her. Jena stands next to Principal Ricky, who is holding her diploma. Her smile is as bright as the sun. She reaches for her diploma, shakes Principal Ricky's hand, and walks off the stage. Jake is called next. Jena turns around to watch Jake get his diploma. His moment seems just as exciting and special as hers. After all diplomas have been given out, Principal Ricky makes a final speech. The crowd cheers, and then hats go up in the air. The moment seems almost overwhelming for Jena. She turns to Jake and gives him the biggest hug ever. Ken, Chance, and Carol can't contain their excitement either, and for the first time in two weeks, everyone seems happy to finally be moving on past high school. Carol gives Jena a big hug, and Ken shakes Jake's hand. Chance and Carol had made up a week before and didn't tell anyone until now. Everything finally seems to be coming together for everyone.

Principal Ricky walks up to Jena. "Jena, I know this has been a tough year for you." He turns to speak to all of them. "But you guys have made it through high school, so be the best you can be as you all go to college. I'm really proud of all of you."

Jena thinks that all these years she has never seen Principal Ricky this way. He isn't just a principal; he is also a nice man, a man who really cares about his students. Mrs. Paterson and Mrs. Parker walk down to where Jena and Jake are standing. Jena hugs her mother. Mrs. Parker tries to whisper in Jena's ear, but her words just won't come out. She just nods her head and leans it next to Jena's. It is like she hasn't heard her mother speak in years. Jena is really hoping to hear her mother's voice, that sweet voice that woke her for school when she was late, that voice that told her father she loved him. Jena longs to hear her speak, but her mother won't say a word. Uncontrollable tears stream down Jena's face from the hurt she knows her mother is still feeling from her father's death. She hugs her mother again just to see if she will say anything, but Mrs. Parker doesn't. She just holds Jena tightly in her arms. Jake hugs the two of them together, and in a second, it seems like everyone is locked in a group hug. Jena hugs Mrs. Paterson. The moment couldn't be more perfect. Yet, Jena thinks for second that this isn't a perfect moment, because her father isn't there to share it with them. Jena doesn't let on to anyone, not even Jake, how much her mother not speaking really hurts her. For weeks now, she's just been acting like an alien had taken over her body. *If I could take away your pain, Mom, I would,* Jena thinks to herself.

Jena tries to brush off her sad thoughts, so she can enjoy the moment. In a few weeks, she will be leaving for college with all her friends. She will be starting a whole new chapter in her life. On the way home, Jena glances out the car window trying to relive the moment she was handed her diploma, the hugs and the emotions that swirled in the air. *What a perfect moment! Nothing could have been more perfect,* Jena thinks to herself, other than her mother speaking again and having both of her parents together holding hands, dancing to their favorite song, or her mom in the kitchen making Dad's favorite *sweet peas.*

CHAPTER TWENTY-TWO

As the days go by, Jena continues to prepare for college. Jake stops every once in awhile to check on her and Mrs. Parker. He often stays for dinner to keep Jena company and preoccupied so she will not worry so much about her mother. Jena feels very guilty leaving her mother in the state she is in. Although Mrs. Parker isn't totally helpless, it is her mother's total silence that worries Jena the most. The first day of college finally nears. Mrs. Parker helps Jena pack the night before. Jena desperately wants to express to her mother how excited she is that she is finally going to college, but she can't.

Mr. and Mrs. Paterson and Jake finally arrive at the house to pick Jena up. Mrs. Parker doesn't want to go. She helps put Jena's stuff in the car, and then she hands Jena a letter. Jena goes to open it, but Mrs. Parker signs not to open it yet. Jena hugs her mother tightly. Mrs. Parker starts to cry.

"Mom, I don't want to leave you," she says. "Not like this."

Mrs. Parker shakes her head and gives Jena a look that says, "You must go. You have to go." And with no words spoken, Jena knows that her mother won't have it any other way. She turns away and gets into the car. Mrs. Parker hugs Mr. and Mrs. Paterson. She reaches over and gives Jake a hug too. Jake kisses her on the cheek. She then walks into the house and closes the door behind her. This will be the last time Jena will see her mother for awhile. She begins to sob softly in the backseat. Jake holds her tightly while Mr. Paterson drives to the college.

"It's going to be all right, Jena," Jake whispers. He grabs Jena's hand and pulls her tightly to him. He tries to comfort her. "Maybe this will turn out to be a good thing, Jena. You're going to college, and you know your mom wouldn't have it any other way." Jake continues to try to comfort her.

Jena sits up. She lets go of Jake's hand and turns to stare out the car window. She turns back to Jake and nods her head in agreement with him. "Maybe you're right," she says in a cracked voice. "Maybe a new beginning will help the both of us." Jena tries to convince herself that everything is going to be all right, that maybe her mother could come back to normal and maybe she would have the time of her life with Jake and her other friends at college, but the certainty of it all still seems so far away from her. Mr. Paterson pulls up to the Northwest University visitor parking lot, and students and parents are everywhere. Flyers and school banners hang all around the university.

"We're here!" Jake yells in an excited voice.

Jake and Jena are the first to get out of the car. Carol is walking around the college campus alone. She walks over to Jake and Jena.

"Hey, guys!" Carol screams and waves.

"Hi." Jena gives Carol a hug. "So I see you made it here too."

"Yeah." Carol looks around in surprise that she got into college. "But I appear to be bit lost," she says.

"Well, it's our first day, Carol, and I'm sure we all will be struggling to find our way around this place," Jake says. He grabs Jena's bags.

Mr. and Mrs. Paterson both get out of the car. "Okay, Mom and Dad," Jake says as he prepares for them to leave, "I think Jena and I can make it from here."

Mrs. Paterson walks up to Jake. "Oh, honey, come on. I'm not going to see you for a while," she says in a teary voice. "You could at least let your mother walk you to your room."

Mr. Paterson hugs Mrs. Paterson closely. "Come on, hon," he says to his wife. "We have to let go someday." Mr. Paterson gently pulls her away from Jake.

She looks up at her husband. "Oh, just one more hug, please." Mrs. Paterson gives Mr. Paterson a quick glare. Jake puts his bags down to give his mother a huge hug. Mrs. Paterson kisses Jake on the cheek and begins to cry. She hugs and squeezes him tight. She can see Jena is about to cry, so she reaches her hand out to her. "Jake will take care of you," she whispers to Jena. "So don't worry, we will look after your mom." Mrs. Paterson blows her nose and wipes her tears with a handkerchief from her purse.

Mr. Paterson wraps his arms around her and comforts her. "Okay, you guys, go on to your rooms and get settled in," he says.

Jena and Jake begin walking away. They wave good-bye. Jake walks Jena to her dorm room. He turns to her. "Well, this is your home for a while." He sets Jena's bags down on her bed.

"Don't put those on my bed, stupid." Jena pushes Jake a little.

"Sorry." Jake puts the bags down on the floor.

A short, black-haired girl stumbles into the room carrying two heavy bags.

"Here, let me help you with that." Jake reaches to help her.

"No, no, no. I can do it myself, thank you!" the girl yells. "I'm a strong woman. I'm a liberated woman, and I don't need a man doing anything for me."

Jake looks back at Jena. "Okay then. Jena, I'm going to go get settled in my room. I'll hook up with you later so we can hang out." Jake turns around. "Oh, by the way, we have orientation today at three, so let's grab some lunch at twelve." Jake walks out of the room.

The freaky girl is talking to herself as she rummages through her bags. Jena looks at her strangely. "Everything all right?" she asks.

The girl looks up and gives Jena an annoyed look. "Yeah, everything is all right. I'm a strong woman," the strange girl repeats. "I know I can do this," she says. "I know I can find what I'm looking for; I just got to keep searching; that's all."

Jena turns away. *Wow, what crazy chick!* she thinks to herself. *And I thought I had problems!* Jena starts unpacking. There is a light knock at the door. Ken is standing in the doorway. Jena looks up at him.

"Hi, Jena," he says. He walks into the room.

"Ken," she replies quickly.

He reaches for her bag. "Need some help unpacking?" he asks.

Jena puts her head down. "No, Ken, I think I got it." He sits down on Jena's bed. She just looks at him.

"What's up, Jena? Are you mad at me?" he asks.

Jena looks up. "No, not at all," she answers politely.

Feeling unwelcome, Ken stands up. Jena's roommate is standing in a corner with her arms folded staring at him. "Okay, well then, I'm going to go hang out," he says. "I guess I'll see you around?"

"Yeah, Ken, I'll see you around," Jena replies. She continues to unpack. Her strange roommate begins rifling through her bags again, searching for this unknown item. Jena unpacks and leaves the room. She tries to close the door behind her. Her strange roommate stops her. She grabs the door before Jena can close it.

"Please. Please, don't close the door right now," the roommates asks.

"What? Why?" Jena asks.

"Because it's not time to close the door," the roommate answers. "The time to close the door is when we're settled in this room and we're ready for the night to end. The day hasn't ended."

Jena stands in shock for moment. "Ah." She is caught off guard. "Okay, well, but when you leave the room, could you close the door anyway, because I really don't want my stuff to be stolen?" Jena asks.

The roommate opens her mouth in shock. "Sure," she answers sharply, rolls her eyes, and then walks away. Jena walks down the halls of the girl's dorm. She explores the other halls.

Chance and Carol are in a hallway talking. Jena tries to walk away without being seen, but Carol spots her. "Jena!" she calls. "Jena, where are you going?"

Trying to not answer, Jena keeps walking.

"Oh, I get it; you were trying to sneak away," Carol tries to make a joke.

"I didn't want to interrupt you guys, since you seem to be in deep conversation."

"Well, we were talking about going to a party after the orientation today," Chance says.

"The orientation is supposed to last at least two hours, but the best is the party right after," Carol says.

"Do you want to go?" Chance asks.

Jena holds her head down. "No, not really guys," Jena answers. "Parties just don't seem to work out that well for us, huh, guys?"

The two girls laugh. "Jena, those were high school parties," Carol replies. "No sweat, chick, we're in college, so the party life here is going to be fun and exciting, not lame like in high school."

Jena puts her hand on her hip. "Carol, it wasn't high school that started the party fights; it was us," she replies. "It was always someone from our group, so no, I'm not going. Let's just start our college friendship off on a good note. No parties."

Jena laughs out loud, and then all three girls laugh together. "I think I'm just going to hang out at the library tonight," Jena answers. "Maybe read some books and then kind of lay low until Monday when the official first day of classes begins."

The girls hug. "Sure, Jena, we understand," Chance says.

"Yeah, no worries, girl." Carol echoes.

"Now that that's settled, Jake and I are meeting for lunch before orientation," Jena says. "Do you guys want to hang out too?"

The girls stare at each other and laugh. "I think we'd rather go to get ready for the party tonight," Carol answers.

"But you have orientation first," Jena says.

"Yeah, we know, but we're going to orientation dressed for the party, so we don't have to come back," Chance says in her happy-girl voice.

The two girls give Jena another hug and walk away to their rooms. Jena goes back to her room. She checks the time on her phone; it's 11:00. She decides to wait for Jake in her room. When Jena reaches the room, she sees the room door is closed. She slowly opens the door, and her strange roommate is hanging up her clothes in her closet.

She turns around. "Oh, you're back." She walks over to greet Jena. Jena looks surprised. "Before you say anything or think I'm crazy," the roommate starts to explain, "I just want to say that I'm hanging up your clothes because I felt you and I got off on the wrong foot earlier, and I just wanted to make peace with you since we're going to be roommates for a while." The roommate puts out her hand. "My name is Theresa."

Jena slowly extends her hand. "My name is Jena. Jena Parker."

"Nice to meet you, Jena Parker."

"The same." Jena smiles. "Nice to meet you too, Theresa. Theresa?" Jena waits for her to say her last name.

Theresa doesn't say anything. She just stares at Jena. "Oh, sorry, my name is Theresa Henderson," Theresa finally answers. "Sorry, I'm not good with making friends." She quickly turns around.

Jena touches her shoulder. "It's okay, Theresa. We'll get to know each other."

Theresa has a contented look on her face. She rushes back over to Jena's closet. "Now before you kill me, do you like your blue pants in the same row as your red ones? Or how about do you like your pants and shirts to be on the same hanger? I know that's weird, but some people are picky, like me." Theresa grins.

Jena stares.

"Well?"

Jena jokes, "That's a complicated question."

The two girls burst out in laughter. They both begin rearranging Jena's clothes in her closet, and just for a moment, Jena forgets her troubles. For moment, her world seems less painful and more forgettable. The two girls help each other rearrange each other's closet. It was a really fun time for Jena. She has made a new friend, and the world doesn't seem as closed to her.

Just maybe, maybe I can live a normul life, Jena thinks to herself.

CHAPTER TWENTY-THREE

Jake came by Jena's room and watched while Jena and Theresa laughed with one another. "You two seemed to be having fun," Jake says. "I guess all the weirdness is over with, huh?"

Jena and Theresa just stare at one another. Jake feels awkward and silly. Jena closes her closet door. She grabs Jake by one arm. "Let's go, silly."

Jake grabs the door-knob to close the door. Jena stops him. "Jake, you can't close the door; the days hasn't ended yet," Jena says.

"What?" Jake replies.

"Never mind, let's just go."

Jake stops in the hallway. "Was I a jerk back there?"

Jena taps one finger against her lips. "Hmm, maybe just a little." She grabs Jake's arm again. "Now let's go eat," she says. "I'm hungry."

Jake pretends to put his ear to Jena's stomach. "Yeah, I can hear the beast rumbling away in there."

Jena and Jake eat lunch at the campus café. The café is crowded with college students. They talk and laugh for hours up until the time for new student orientation. They both walk to where the orientation is to take place. When they arrive, the three-hundred-seat auditorium is almost full. Jake and Jena find a seat in the back of the room. They pass Ken on the way up to their seats. Ken smiles at Jena and nods at Jake. Five minutes before the orientation starts, Chance and Carol stand in the doorway showing off their skimpy outfits. Dean Philips stands in front of the class with an old gray suit on. His glasses hang off the tip of his nose. He looks down through his glasses, his eyes patrolling the auditorium to politely signal to the two girls to please find a seat so that the orientation can begin.

Chance and Carol take advantage of having the entire room watching them as they find a seat. They walk slowly and seductively in order to get attention from all who are watching, which is just about everyone in the room. The dean's eyes follow Chance and Carol as well. Two guys in the front row can't contain their excitement for the two girls and stand up to offer them their seats.

"Welcome, new Northwest students. Hello, everyone, and welcome. I'm Dean Philips." Dean Philips's voice echoes throughout the entire room. "Welcome to your first day at an outstanding university."

The orientation lasts for hours. Various student orientation instructors speak. They talk about the university and take questions from the students. There are laughs and school spirit cheers. The sound of the instructor's voice starts to fade away for Jena. Her thoughts drift to her mother and how lonely she must be feeling alone in the house all by herself. Jena feels guilty for leaving her mother alone. Five o'clock finally comes, but the instructor is still talking. Chance's and Carol's patience is beginning to wear thin, thinking about how boring this orientation is and all the fun they are going to have at the party. The final instructor finally speaks and wraps up the orientation. The students are released.

One student yells out, "Let's party!"

Everyone cheers. Each sorority and fraternity group has planned their own party. Chance and Carol stay seated to be the last to leave the room. What they really want is what they get: every male student staring at them and every female student envying them. Ken stops to try to speak to Chance, but she ignores him. Carol smiles at him. He walks away with the crowd. Jake and Jena get up to leave.

"Are you going to any of the sorority parties, Jena?" Jake asks.

"No. I think I'm going to spend my evening at the library," Jena replies.

"Library?" Jake responds in a disappointed voice. "Jena, we will have plenty of time to study; let's go hang out and have a good time." Jake insists. "I really would like to spend some time with you." He gives Jena a sad look.

"No, you go and have fun," she says. "I'm not in the mood for a party. Like I said, I'm going to the library."

"Well, I'll go too," Jake tries to respond.

"Alone," Jena replies.

Jake is disappointed, but he tries not to show Jena how much. Jena starts walking out of the orientation room. "I'm just going to call my mom really quick and then head to the library. I'll catch up with you later, Jake." She reaches for his hand. Jake nods his head in a disappointed way.

"Sure," Jake says. "I understand. But, Jena, please don't shut me out. I'm here for you."

Jena smiles. "I know, Jake." She walks out.

Chance and Carol finally get up. Several guys are waiting for them. They just soak up all the attention they are getting from the guys. They walk away with ten to twelve male students following them. Jena walks slowly to the campus library. There are only the librarian and two other students in the entire building. She walks to the literature section. She picks up a book and begins reading it. Four hours has passed without Jena noticing. And at nine o'clock, the librarian taps Jena on the shoulder.

"Hi," the librarian whispers in the lowest voice Jena has ever heard. Jena moves closer to hear what she's saying. "The library is now closed."

Jena nods her head okay. She looks around and sees the library is completely empty. Trying to speak as softly, Jena barely moves her lips or makes a sound. "Yes, ma'am." Jena leaves. Outside the library, it's dark and cold. The wind is blowing briskly. Jena tries to bundle her jacket as tightly as she can. She forgets the exact way to her dorm. She walks down a path that looks familiar to her. Three guys are standing outside talking. Their faces aren't clear to Jena. She just keeps on walking. The boys follow her. Jena tries to run. One of the boys grabs her, and then they all drag her behind the library building. Jena screams, "Help!" No one hears her. One of the boys stuffs her mouth with something to shut her up. He punches Jena in the face twice. She becomes dizzy, almost unconscious. Dark figures are all Jena can see. Her vision is blurred. One of the boys is wearing strong cologne, something she had never smelled before. The strong odor from the cologne is all Jena can smell besides the alcohol on their breaths. Their hands are mostly rough; one of them is soft. The wind howling and the depths of her fear grow but dim away as she fades in and out of consciousness. The boys never say a word; they just hand gesture as if they know exactly what each is to do. While two boys hold Jena down, the other two take turns, two savage beasts invading her most precious place. The one who seems to be the leader cuts Jena's pants. He rips her pants off, removes her panties, and begins brutally raping her. The boys take turns raping Jena. Tears run down one of her swollen eyes. Panting is all Jena hears before she completely passes out. The boys leave her there unconscious and with her clothes ripped off. She lays there bleeding and cold, so cold that her body is numbed.

Jena's roommate reports her missing, and that's when campus police find her behind the library raped, unconscious, and unaware of her surroundings. Campus police immediately call for an ambulance. Late in the night and into the early morning, Jena is transported to the nearest emergency room. Jena lies on the hospital stretcher with one eyed beaten closed. The bright light from the hospital lights burns her eyes. With one closed completely, she keeps the other closed tightly to help stop the stinging and burning from her tears.

CHAPTER TWENTY-FOUR

Jena can vaguely hear what is going on around her. The nurse gives her a shot. "It's okay, Jena; you're in the hospital, and we're going to take good care of you," the nurse says.

Jena can feel herself drifting away, far away to a place she is all too familiar with.

She is back on the airplane standing in the middle of the aisle. She's wearing a red leather coat and red hat and gripping a knife tightly in her hand. All of the men on the airplane are still faceless, reading newspapers and smoking cigars. Mr. McNeil sits in the back still reading his paper. Jena walks up to him. "I see you're still here," she says.

Mr. McNeil looks up through his glasses. "Why are you bothering me, ma'am? What have I done to you?" Mr. McNeil asks. "I've done nothing that I know of." Jena stands closer to him. She puts the knife to his neck. Mr. McNeil sits still. "Please, please, don't kill me whoever you are," Mr. McNeil pleads for his life.

All of the faceless men turn to stare at Jena. Jena puts down the knife. She walks with briskness and confidence back to the front of the plane. She holds the knife in next to her side. Each of the faceless men put their newspaper down as she passes. Their eyes focus on her and then back on Mr. McNeil. The men speak simultaneously to Mr. McNeil. "Do you know who she is?"

"She's Jena."

Jena slowly tries to wake up from the dream when she hears a voice. "Jena?" a nurse calls. "Jena, hi, I'm Elaine. I'm your nurse." Jena slowly opens one of her eyes. "Jena, you're in the hospital. Something really awful has happened to you, but we are taking very good care of you. Jena, if you understand what I'm saying, please lift a finger from either hand." Jena lifts her right index finger. "Great," the nurse replies. "Jena, we want to contact someone from your family, but we don't have a number or any information. I know you probably don't want to talk right now, but I'm sure your mother, father, or someone would like to know where you are and how you're doing."

Jena sits silent for moment. She blinks one eye. She slowly tries to speak. "Don't," Jena whispers in a cracked and wounded voice.

"Jena, I can't hear you," the nurse replies.

"Don't," Jena tries to speak again. "Don't call anyone, please."

The nurse stands still for a moment. "I understand," Nurse Elaine replies.

Nurse Elaine leaves Jena's room. She falls back to sleep and begins to dream again. This time, she's standing in the middle of nowhere.

There's fog everywhere. Someone taps her on her shoulder. Jena turns around. A foot away from her stands her father. He stands in the middle of the fog. Jena runs to him and hugs him tightly.

"Dad, I'm so happy to see you," she says.

Mr. Parker stands without saying anything. Jena pulls back to look at him. He smiles at her. "Dad, are we in heaven? I know you're in heaven. Where else could you be?" Jena asks. Mr. Parker begins to back away. Jena tries to follow, but her body can't move. "Dad, please don't go!" Jena cries out. "Please don't go!" Jena cries out again, but Mr. Parker fades away in the fog. "Dad!" Jena screams out loud. Her voices echo through the dark. "Dad!"

Jake stands over Jena's bed and sees her struggling in her dream. He touches her lightly. "Jena!" he calls. "Jena, wake up! Jena, you're dreaming! Wake up," Jake says.

Jena stares at Jake. She looks away, ashamed. Tears stream down her face. "Jake, go away." Jena turns away. "Please just go away," Jena says.

"Jena, I know you might not want to see anyone right now, but I'm not leaving you," Jake says. Jena keeps her face turned away from Jake. She cries and reaches out for his hand. Jake kisses hers. "It's all right," Jake says as he kisses and caresses Jena's hand. He begins to cry. "Jena, it's all right. I'm here for you. I'm going to find out who did this to you, and I'm going to kill them. I'm going to kill them, Jena." Jena screams out uncontrollably. Jake runs to get the nurse.

Nurse Elaine and the two doctors run into Jena's room. Jake walks quickly out of Jena's room. Jena is yelling, "Let me out." She tries to tear out the needles and oxygen tube connected to her.

"Ms. Parker, please calm down," one says, trying to hold Jena down.

Another nurse comes in quickly and injects medicine into her arm. Jake, frantic, stands in the doorway and watches. He starts pacing back and forth past her room door. Jena begins to calm down slowly. Her body relaxes back into her bed. Her eyes slowly close, and then she falls completely out into a deep sleep. Nurse Elaine fixes Jena's oxygen tube and puts her IV needle back in. Jake walks back into the room.

"She should rest comfortably now," Nurse Elaine says. "Maybe you should come back in a few days to allow her to adjust to what has happened to her. Do you know who her parents are?" Nurse Elaine asks.

"Yes, I do," Jake replies.

"She doesn't want the hospital to contact her parents, but she really needs to have someone here for her."

Jake wipes the tears from his eyes. "Jena's father was murdered not too long ago, and her mother is not well right now," he answers. "I'm her only family." Jake stares at Nurse Elaine. "The only person she can count on right now." Jake walks over to Jena's bedside. "I'm going to stay here with her for as long as it takes. I'm going to leave now, but I'll be back with my bags."

Nurse Elaine can hear the hurt in Jake's voice. "I'll be here for her until she recovers." He begins to cry again. "I'll be here for her forever." Jake stands up from the chair.

Nurse Elaine walks out of the room with tears in her eyes. She closes the door behind her to give Jake some privacy.

Days and weeks go by. Jake comes to the hospital when Jena is asleep and awake. Sometimes, Jena will cry in her sleep, cry for help, and then she'll fall back to sleep as if she somehow finally manages to find a peaceful place. While awake, Jena won't speak a word to anyone, not even Jake. Day by day, Jena gets better, but her silence worries Jake because he just can't reach her to bring her back to the Jena he knew. He can't reach her. The police come to Jena's room to try to talk to her, but she won't say a word.

One night, after Jena has been in the hospital for over a month, she is lying awake staring at the wall in her room while Jake is asleep. Jena quietly arises from her bed. She slips on her clothes and packs the few items that belong to her. She drapes her bag over her shoulder and watches Jake as he sleeps soundly in the chair. She slips away from the hospital without being noticed by anyone. In the middle of the night, Jena heads back to her dorm room to get some cash she had hidden in her closet. When she enters the room, her roommate Theresa is asleep. Theresa suddenly wakes.

"Jena, what are you doing out of the hospital?" Theresa asks. She removes the covers and walks over to Jena. Jena doesn't say a word. "Jena, are you all right?"

Jena goes straight to her closet and begins searching for her hidden cash. She grabs her hats and pulls out the hidden money. The letter her mother gave her falls off a shelf in her closet to the floor; she slowly picks it up and puts it in her bag. Theresa quickly switches on the room lights.

"Turn off the lights!" Jena screams.

Theresa just stares in shock. Jena looks up at her and then stands up. "Now!" she screams. Theresa rushes to turn off the lights. "Jena, you're really freaking me out." Theresa panics. "I mean you come here in the middle of the night. You're not talking." Theresa begins to cry. "What's going on?"

Jena turns to Theresa and gives her a chilling, eerie look. "You might want to stay out of my way," she says abruptly. She gives Theresa an evil look, opens the door, and then walks out of the room.

CHAPTER TWENTY-FIVE

Jena thinks to herself as she walks out of her dorm room. She catches a cab to take her somewhere, anywhere. She stares out the cab window thinking about her rape. Her thoughts zone in and out, and a voice in her head speaks to her. *"Are you cold? Do you feel a chill running through your bones that makes you stand so still as if you're lifeless? Almost dead. Frozen. Sometimes, that's what I feel when I think of what he did to me. How he changed my life in a way that I will never be the same again."*

The cabdriver is impatient. "Where to, lady?" he asks.

Jena gives him a blank glare. "Take me to the nearest hotel."

"You got it," he answers.

Jena gets out and pays the cabdriver. She walks through the front door and drops her bag on the counter. There's a fat man eating a hotdog with mustard running down his cheeks to his shirt. Jena watches with disgust. Jena clears her thought. The TV is loud, and the hotel clerk is yelling at it while watching his favorite show, *Fat Slobs Are People Too*.

"Ah, look at that jerk?" a voice in Jena's head says.

The clerk throws his French fries at the television and begins to scream, "Who does this asshole thinks he is? Fat people need love too."

Jena rings the bell on the counter. The man just sits and ignores her. She continues to ring the bell. Finally acknowledging Jena, he says, "Just a minute." He raises one finger up at Jena, but he doesn't look at her. She gives him a deep, dark stare.

You lazy piece of shit. Low life. Creep, she thinks to herself.

Finally, he struggles to stand up out of the chair. He appears to weigh about three hundred pounds, and his shirt barely covers his stomach as his jeans pants sag in back. Jena rolls her eyes and then grabs her bag from off the counter.

"Well, hello there, young lady," he says, trying to flirt. He raises one of his eyebrows at Jena. There is mustard spattered all over his shirt. Jena fixates on the mustard. Trying to wipe the mustard off his shirt, he says, "I like your red hat." He leans over the counter. "It's hot."

Jena looks up at the man. She doesn't blink. "How much for a room?"

He tries to prolong the conversation. "Well, we have all sorts of different types of rooms, especially for a pretty lady like you. Just about any size … you like." He tries to lean back so Jena can look at his personal area. "What size would you like?"

Jena puts money on the counter. "Anything," Jena replies.

"Well, I have a cozy room on the second floor. It'll give a whole lot of privacy, if you know what I mean." The clerk smiles at Jena.

"Hmmm …" she mumbles.

"That will be thirty dollars, little lady."

"All I have is twenty-five," she says.

"I'll take it." he hands her the room keys.

Jena begins walking out the door. The man tries to push his way around the corner. "Hey, we got cable and coffee … and breakfast in the morning," he says, breathing hard, as Jena walks out. Jena doesn't turn around or wait for him to finish. She walks to her room, puts down her bag, and turns the television to the news. She paces up and down the hotel room listening to the news. There is a knock at Jena's hotel room door. Jena pulls the curtain back. The front desk clerk is standing at the door holding a wine bottle and two glasses. She gets angry but opens the door. The fat clerks stands in the doorway.

"Hi, it's me again, you know, the front-desk guy," he says.

Jena just stares. He starts to walk in, but Jena stops him. "Well, we aren't much of a hotel here, but we do like to show our guest good hospitality." He hands Jena the wine bottle and a glass. Looking into Jena's room, he asks, "Can I come in?"

Jena hesitates at first but then backs away to let him in. She snatches the wine bottle out of the clerk's hand and opens it with her teeth. "Oh, you're quick." The clerk strolls into the room. His butt crack is showing. Despite Jena being angry, she pretends not to care and just pours the clerk a glass of wine and then herself some. She puts the wine bottle on the table.

Trying to make conversation, he asks, "So are you from around here?"

"No," Jena replies. "I'm just passing through."

The clerk flops himself onto Jena's bed. She pushes out her lips in disgust. "We have nice, comfortable beds here." The clerk pats his hand on the bed. "Why don't you lie down next to me and check it out?" Jena walks toward the bathroom. "Hey, where are you going?" the clerk asks.

Jena turns on the water in the tub, takes off all of her clothes, and then stands naked in the bathroom doorway. The clerk's eyes widen. He begins to chuckle. "I see you and I are going to be good friends. Huh?" He struggles to get off the bed. The fat clerk undresses and rubs one of Jena's breasts on his way into the bathroom. "You're nice and firm. I like that," he says in a panting voice. Jena pretends to be excited.

"Why don't get in the tub and I'll join you?" she says.

The clerk gets more excited by touching Jena. "Oh, you're nice and firm," he says over again.

He turns to get into the tub. Jena pushes him hard. He slips, falls, and hits his head on the toilet. The clerk's head is busted and bleeding. "What the hell? Help me." He reaches out for Jena's hand. She walks back into the bedroom, reaches for the lamp, removes the shade, and then walks back into the bathroom. The clerk tries to scream louder, but Jena begins beating him on the head over and over again. Blood spurts from the clerk's head and splatters all over Jena's body and the bathroom. Jena continues to hit him over and over again. The clerk's body slumps in the corner of the bathroom. Blood from his head spills out furiously. Jena puts the lamp down. She's breathing hard with no expression on her face. Then she begins to smile while staring at the clerk's cold, lifeless body lying on the floor. She kneels down to touch the streaming blood on the floor. Staring at the blood reminds her of the night her father died. She whispers to the dead clerk, "You go now. You go now, and tell somebody." She stands and poses her body firmly. "You go and tell Mr. McNeil I'm coming." The water in the tub is almost overflowing. Jena turns off the water. She steps over the dead clerk and gets into the tub to take a bath. Then she dresses and leaves the clerk dead in the room.

***

At the hospital, Jake sleeps through the night. He awakes the next morning and finds Jena's bed empty. He walks down to the nurses' station. Nurse Elaine is working on clinical papers. Jake walks up to the counter.

"Hi, does Jena have some tests? Because she's not in the room, and I was just wondering ..." Jake asks.

The nurse reviews Jena's chart. "No, none that I ...I'm aware of," Nurse Elaine stutters. She begins checking all of the clinics for appointments for Jena. She calls security to the floor, but no one can find her. "Jake, I believe that Jena may be gone," Nurse Elaine says in an uncertain tone. "I guess she slipped out in the middle of the night."

Jake runs back to Jena's room and then outside the hospital. He frantically searches for Jena everywhere. Jake goes back to the college to search for Jena. He goes to her room. Theresa is just leaving. "Theresa, have you seen Jena?" Jake asks.

Theresa just stands still, afraid to answer.

"Theresa, answers me!" Jake yells.

"Jake, she was here last night." Theresa pauses. "She's not herself." She begins walking, almost running, away. "Look, I have to go, but you need to find her and help her. She really needs help." Theresa walks quickly away. Jake speaks to anyone he can find to find out if anyone has seen Jena. He calls Mrs. Parker, but she doesn't answer the phone. He finally goes to the police department to report Jena as a missing person.

CHAPTER TWENTY-SIX

Jena takes a cab to the train station. There are hundreds of people there. She waits to board the train that will take her home, take her back to a place where pain lies waiting for her, to a house where her father once lived and loved and where her mother once spoke and lived a life with meaning and hope. The idea of going home to see her mother made her feel good and bad at the same time.

There in the graveyard will be my father. And the man who killed him still walks free—free to kill again and free to make me feel unfree, she thinks to herself. Jena boards the train. She shares a car with a traveling doctor, a tall, slim, old man who carries a medical bag with him everywhere. He sits across from Jena reading a newspaper. His glasses hang from the tip of his nose, and he snuffles to suggest he has allergies. Jena stares out the train's window. The old doctor continues reading his paper. The doctor puts his paper down. Jena is staring at him.

"Is there something wrong, young lady?" the doctor asks.

"No," Jena answers quietly and then looks back out the window.

Feeling a little uneasy, the doctor clears his throat. "So what's your name, young lady, and where are you headed?" he asks in a curious voice.

Jena continues to stare out the window for a moment and then looks back at the doctor. "My name is Jena." She pauses for second. She knows she is no longer the innocent young lady who laughed and felt sorry for things she couldn't change. She doesn't feel sorry anymore. She isn't even sure if she feels anything at all. She just knows she isn't the same person and will never be again. "My name is Jena." Jena pauses. "Jena Gray. I'm going home to see my mother."

"Ah, home," the old doctor replies. "You must be a college student." Fixing his paper, he says, "Well, I'm sure your mother will be very excited to see you."

Jena nods. "Yes, she'll be very excited."

"Well, I guess it's not a secret with me carrying this bag and all, that I'm a doctor. I've been practicing medicine for over fifty years. So what are you studying in college? What do you want to do when you graduate?" he asks.

All Jena can think about is finding and killing Mr. McNeil. "I don't know what I want to do," she answers. "Not yet." Jena gets an angry look on her face.

Feeling Jena's uneasiness, the doctor backs off on asking Jena any more questions and begins reading his paper again. The old man begins to slump to get comfortable in his chair. Jena just stares at him with a devious look. She stares at his medical bag. The old man dozes off to sleep. Jena watches him. She reaches for his medical bag. In the bag, there are all sorts of medical instruments, pills, and a sharp cutting medical knife. Jena removes the pills and the knife, and she watches while the old man sleeps peacefully. The newspaper he had been reading lies on his lap. Jena looks the doctor up and down. She wonders what he's dreaming about or if he's even dreaming at all. *He's been a doctor for fifty years. I wonder how many deaths he's seen or caused.* She stabs him in the stomach while he sleeps. The doctor bleeds out quickly. Jena watches as he bleeds to death. He wakes briefly.

"Are you cold?" he whispers to Jena. "Is it cold on this train?"

Jena sits across from him and just stares. "Yes," she answers. "It is very cold on this train."

The old man closes his eyes and dies. The last hours of the train ride, Jena sits watching the old man's dead body. Blood drips from his stomach to the floor. The old man lies still with his mouth slightly open. His glasses hang from his nose while his body sways back and forth with the train's movement. Jena wonders how a body can still move even when it is dead. She thinks to herself, *I'm still moving, and I believe I'm dead too.*

The train stops. Jena is finally home. She grabs her bag and leaves the old man's dead body lying in the train car. A cab takes her home. Mrs. Parker is in the house watching television. Jena rings the doorbell. Mrs. Parker opens the door, and Jena rushes into her mother's arms. "Mom,"

Jena says gratefully. Mrs. Parker doesn't say a word, but Jena can tell that she is happy to see her. Mrs. Parker touches Jena's face gently. The smile on her face is like Christmas to Jena. Jena walks into the house, and everything seems the same. She feels so relieved. The living room, kitchen, and even her room—nothing has changed. Jena feels peace for the moment. She feels right being home. Her family picture still hangs on her dresser mirror. The breeze from her window is still flowing. Everything seems perfect, but everything isn't perfect. Out of Jena's room window, she can see the McNeils' house. Her mother still isn't speaking, and the haunting memories of the night her father was murdered make it seem like it was yesterday. The horrible feeling of that night her father was killed comes rushing back to Jena instantly. The breeze that once felt warm now feels cold and empty. Jena lies on her bed for the moment, and then she goes downstairs. Mrs. Parker is in the kitchen trying to make dinner. Jena walks up to her. "Mom, are you ever going to speak again?"

Mrs. Parker stares at Jena with disappointed eyes. She shakes her head with uncertainty and then walks up to Jena to hold her. "Mom, you have to speak to me," Jena says. "I need you to speak to me. So much has happened since I left home, and now more than ever, I need the comfort of my mother." Mrs. Parker can see the hurt in Jena's eyes. She tries to speak.

"What's ..." Mrs. Parker tries to speak again. "What's wrong ...?"

Jena can tell her mother is trying to speak, but how can she tell her that she's just been raped and that she's killed two people. How would her mother understand? Could she even cope with any more pain in her life? Mrs. Parker rushes to grab a piece of paper and pen. She writes quickly on the paper. "What's wrong, Jena?" Mrs. Parker stares at Jena.

Jena doesn't say a word, but the tears begin to stream from her eyes.

Mrs. Parker grabs her. She struggles to speak again. "What's wrong?" Mrs. Parker holds Jena tightly. Through Jena's pain, the sound of her mother's struggling voice makes her feel some happiness. Finally hearing her mother's voice reminds her of when she was a kid and her mother would speak to her all the time, helping with her homework, making dinner, and most of all, talking to Dad. Watching her mother struggle to speak, Jena doesn't have the heart to tell her mother the truth.

"Don't worry, Mom." Jena touches her mother's face. "Everything will be all right. I just miss Dad; that's all."

Mrs. Parker smiles and nods to say, "Me too."

"Now let's see what you're cooking." Mrs. Parker smiles.

Jena puts her arms around her mother's shoulders. They sit, eat, and mostly Jena talks throughout the evening. Mrs. Parker manages to say a few words here and there, but the happiness on her face is more than enough for Jena. This is one of the best nights for the both of them. They laugh at family pictures and even play a game. "Mom, you look tired," Jena says. "Why don't you go up and get ready for bed, and I'll clean up down here," Jena says as she looks around the kitchen.

Mrs. Parker heads upstairs. Jena stands and stares at the bottom of the stairway and watches while her mother slowly walks up. "I'll come up and talk to you before I go to bed, Mom." Mrs. Parker turns around, gives Jena a slight smile, and then nods her head.

CHAPTER TWENTY-SEVEN

Downstairs is quiet. The still of the night fills the room as Jena stands and stares off at an old antique her grandmother had given her mother when she was a little girl. *How old and precious that antique is to Mother,* Jena thinks to herself. *How much she loves it and how heartbroken she would be if anything were to happen to it.* Jena sits down on the couch in the living room. *How soft this couch feels,* she thinks to herself. Suddenly, a crackling sound comes from upstairs.

Mrs. Parker is walking around getting ready for bed. Jena flashes back to the last time she saw her father, just before he was killed. That horrible night comes rushing back to her, and all she can think about is the look on her mother's face after her father was shot and murdered. Jena rises from the couch and walks up to the old antique that Grandmother gave her mother. She touches it gently. She stares at it and wonders what her mother would think if she broke the antique. Just above that antique was the family photo of her mother, father, and herself smiling as if nothing could go wrong. *Yet, at this very moment, everything that could be wrong is wrong,* Jena thinks. Jena reaches in her coat pocket. She grabs the pills she stole from the doctor on the train, and then walks to the kitchen. Mom always loved a glass of warm milk before she went to bed. Jena thinks back to when her mother made her warm milk to help her sleep. She makes her mother a tall glass of warm milk and then walks upstairs. Mrs. Parker is lying in her bed almost asleep. Jena walks into the room with the glass in her hand. Mrs. Parker slowly awakens and sits up in the bed with a smile of joy on her face like a little child when a mother comes to tuck her in. As she walks toward her mother's bedside with the glass of milk in her hand, her parents' favorite song repeats over and over in her head. "If I Can't Have You, I Don't Want Nobody Else, Baby."

"If I can't have you," Jena begins to sing the song to her mother as she walks toward her. "If I can't have you, I don't want nobody, baby. If I can't have you ..."

"Ah, oh," Mrs. Parker is thrilled. Jena continues to sing her and her father's favorite love song. Jena sits down on the edge of her mother's bed and hands her the glass of warm milk. Mrs. Parker begins drinking the milk. Jena watches with silence in her eyes. She drinks all the milk and then puts the glass on the table next to her bed. Her eyes instantly begin to get very heavy.

"I love you, Mom," Jena whispers quietly to her mother. Mrs. Parker tries to stay awake. "I know how much you loved Dad." Her body begins to go limp. "I know that your life will never be the same without him." Jena rubs her mother's hair and face as she lies there. Mrs. Parker tries to reach for Jena, but her body is very weak from the pills. "I remember the painful look on your face, Mom, when you knew Daddy was gone forever. It is a look I will never forget." Mrs. Parker goes quietly and peacefully into a deep sleep that she will never wake from. Jena watches as her mother drifts away. She had laced her mother's milk with a sedative she found in the doctor's medical bag.

"Good-bye, Mother," Jena says while she covers her mother's body with a blanket. "You go now," Jena says. "You go and you tell him. You tell him I'm coming for him." She kisses her on the forehead and walks downstairs to clean the kitchen. She cleans the entire kitchen and even cleans up the living room. On her way out, she grabs her bag and then takes one last look upstairs where she knows her mother lies dead. "Tell Dad I said hello and that I love him," Jena says as she turns to open the front door to leave. She leaves all the lights on. As she opens the door, Jake is just beginning to ring the doorbell. Surprised, Jena stands still in the doorway.

"Jena!" Jake calls as he grabs her body tightly in his arms. "Are you all right?" he asks.

"I'm fine, Jake," she says. "What are you doing here?" she asks.

"I'm looking for you," Jake replies in a concerned voice. "I've been so worried. I mean you left the hospital without saying a thing to me. Why? The hospital's looking for you too." Jena stares upstairs. "What's going on, Jena?" Jake asks. Jake looks past Jena into the house and up the stairs. "Is your mother all right?" he asks.

Jena walks out and stands on the porch with the door open signaling for Jake to follow. Jake walks out. Jena closes the door. "Yes, she's fine," Jena replies. "She's asleep though, and I don't want to disturb her, so why don't we leave and go somewhere?"

"Somewhere?" Jake answers. "Where?"

"I don't know, just anywhere but here," Jena says. She glares across the street toward the McNeils' house.

Jake turns and looks too. "I understand," he says. He wraps his arm around Jena, and they walk back to the car.

Jake opens the door for her, and Jena sits down quickly in the car. She takes one last glance at the house she called home as Jake drives away. She turns to him. "Jake, let's go to New York."

Jake pulls over to the side of the road. "Jena, New York?" Jake acts surprised.

"Yes, New York," she replies. "I want to get away to somewhere new and exciting. All you have to do is drive me there, and then you can come back." Jena gets a little angry. "If you don't take me, I'll find a way to go anyway."

Jake pulls back onto the highway. "Jena, you know I'll do anything for you." Jake turns to her. "I'll take you, and I'll stay with you as long as you need me to. Besides, there's no class this week."

Jake drives all night to New York. Jena barely speaks to him. They arrive in New York, and the streets are still lit up. Jake and Jena stare at the Statue of Liberty in amazement.

"I think I'll try this hotel," he says. He gets out of the car. "You wait here, Jena. Let me check this place out." Jake pays for a week's stay at the nice hotel. They are both exhausted from the long drive. "Are you hungry, Jena?" he asks. Jena nods her head yes. "You can go up and get settled in the room, and I'll go get us some food."

"Okay," Jena replies.

"Do you want me to take your bag in first?" Jake reaches for Jena's bag.

Jena grabs it quickly. "I got it, Jake," she says abruptly.

"Okay, well then, I'll be back shortly."

Jake hands her the key to the room. She walks in and hides her bag under the bed and then lies down on the bed. Mentally exhausted, Jena falls asleep on the bed.

She is back on the airplane still wearing the red leather jacket and the red hat. Mr. McNeil is at the back of the airplane still reading his paper. Jena walks up to him again. She puts the knife back to his neck. He panics. "Why are you doing this?" Mr. McNeil asks. "What do you want from me?"

Jena looks closely into Mr. McNeil's face. "I want you to die," she answers. "I want you to bleed like you made him bleed."

Mr. McNeil starts to sweat. "Who are you talking about?" he asks.

Before she can answer, she wakes up and stares up at the ceiling of the room. Jake knocks on the door. She opens it, and he's standing in the doorway with two greasy bags in his hand. The bags are dripping. "Did you kill something?" she asks. "It's about time you got back," Jena says as she swings the door open. She grabs Jake and gives him a kiss on the lips.

"Let's go shopping?" Jena asks.

Jake is surprised but is secretly delighted by Jena's sudden attention to him. He puts the bags on the table. "I thought you were hungry?" he asks.

"I am." Jena grabs one of the bags, pulls out a sandwich, and then takes a bite. "But I want to go shopping," she says. She turns around and around in the room "This is New York; there's shopping everywhere." She stops and stares at Jake. "So let's go." Jena pulls Jake's arm.

He grabs a sandwich and takes a bite as Jena pulls him out of the hotel room. "We're in New York, Jake." She starts to giggle as she glances over at him. "This is the place, Jake, where you can start over, where anyone can get a second chance."

Jake is mesmerized by Jena. His love for her is obvious. Just watching her happiness makes him feel good inside. Jena's sudden burst of excitement thrills Jake. He can't wait to take her shopping. He would do anything to make her happy again. They go to several stores. Jena buys shoes and a purse, but she can't find the perfect dress. "Jake, I want to find the perfect dress." She is just about to give up. Jake stops to look at hats from a vendor parked on the sidewalk. Jena leans against a building disappointed. "I want the perfect dress," Jena says out loud.

Cars pass back and forth on the busy street. People are walking around everywhere. Across the street in the window is a dress. Jena stands up straight. She smiles as she looks across the street at the dress that is displayed in the boutique window. *I've found you,* she thinks. "I've finally found you."

CHAPTER TWENTY-EIGHT

Jena runs across the street without thinking. Cars honk their horns, but she doesn't care; she just keeps running. Jake chases her, trying not to get hit by a car. Jena stands in front of the boutique window. Her eyes glaze over as she stares at the dress in the window. She turns to Jake. "Jake, this is it! This is the dress I've been hoping for." A red dress is displayed on a mannequin in the window. The dress sways close to the mannequin's body. The front hangs low, and the dress fits close and has a mermaid shape. Jena walks into the store. An old woman sits on a stool waiting for a customer.

"Hello and welcome," the old woman says in an eager voice. Jena stands and stares at the dress. The old woman struggles to stand up. "How may I help you, young lady?" she says slowly.

Pointing at the dress in the window, Jena says, "I want that dress. The red one in the window. I want it."

"Oh, that dress," the old woman replies.

"Yes, please; I have to have it," Jena says.

The old woman walks toward the window. "Well, that's the only one I have. Nobody has ever tried it on. If you want it, I'll sell it to you, and I'll even throw in that red hat from over there." The old woman points to a red hat that hangs on a hat rack. Jena walks slowly toward the hat. She touches it. The hat is a high-top shape. Jena puts it on her head and then stands in front of the mirror. The old lady and Jake stand next to her and look in the mirror. "See, that hat fits you perfectly."

Jena stares at herself in the mirror. A flashback from her dream of her wearing a red hat crosses her mind. "Yes, it does," Jena says.

The old woman walks away to get the dress off the mannequin. "Let me help you, ma'am," Jake says. Jake removes the mannequin from the window. He takes it in the back. The old woman follows. "I thought I'd bring her back here," he says. "I don't want her naked in the window."

The old woman smiles. "You're nice, kid." Then she gives Jake a long stare. "But be careful," she tells him like a fortune-teller.

Jake pays for the dress and hat. Standing out in front of the store, Jake holds Jena's hand. "Are you happy?" he asks.

"Yes, I'm so happy, Jake," Jena says and kisses him on the cheek.

"Now can we eat?" Jake asks.

"Of course, let's go," Jena replies.

Walking on the streets of New York, Jena feels bold, empowered. *There are so many people in New York,* she thinks. *So many people like me, people who are confused, happy at times, maybe they have someone they love, someone like a father or a mother.* A woman passes Jena and stares at her in a fearful way. Jena mumbles to herself. *And even someone who may have killed. Killed just like me. They all are maybe just like me. Searching for something. Something we don't know even exists.*

"Here." Jena stops in front of a café. "This is where we'll eat."

Jake takes a peek inside. "Looks decent," he says. He opens the door for Jena, and they walk in. A man seats them at a table. Two kids around their same age sit next to them at a table. "Dude, we're in New York and that club is hot," one of the guys says.

Jena listens in on their conversation. "Are you sure, man?" the other guy asks. "Because if there's not a lot of hot women there, I'm going to kick your ass."

They both start laughing. A tall, slender waitress walks up to Jake and Jena's table. "What'll you have?" she asks in a rough Jersey accent.

Jake looks at Jena. Jena shrugs her shoulders. Jake feels a little intimidated. "We'll take the special with two Cokes. All right?" Jake says.

"Two specials, Earl," the waitress yells as she walks away.

She brings back the food. The two guys get up from the table. Jena stops one of them. "So where's the party tonight, guys?" she asks. "I overheard you talking about a club."

"Yeah, it's supposed to be hot. It's called New House Club," one of the guys answers.

The other guy stares at Jena and smiles. "You guys should come." He winks at Jena. Jake gives him a jealous look. The two guys leave.

"So what do you say, Jake? Up for a little clubbing tonight?"

Jake stares into Jena's eyes. He can't say no. He takes a bite of his sandwich. His cell phone vibrates. "That's weird," he says.

"What's weird?" Jena asks.

"My mom called, but I didn't even hear the phone ring the first time. I should get this."

"No." Jena grabs the phone. "Let's just have some fun."

The phone stops ringing. Jena hands him back the phone.

"Looks like she left a message, but I'll check it later."

"Yeah, check it later," Jena replies. She starts to eat and smiles at Jake. "I'm sure she'll understand. So what about tonight?" Jena asks again.

"Why not?" Jake replies. In his mind, all he can think about is how much he loves her and that every moment spent with her is all he has ever wanted. "I'm out of school for a week, and hell, we're in New York," he answers. "So why not have some fun?"

Everything seems great between Jake and Jena. Jake is starting to believe that Jena will make it through her problems. She seems happy for the first time since the death of her father and the horrible rape she endured. Jake never brings up the rape because he wants her to forget about it. All he wants is to be close to her, to see her smile, and to fantasize about her. *I want to love, Jena,* he thinks to himself. *I'm so in love with you.*

Back at the hotel, Jake dozes off in a chair while watching TV. Jena watches over him while he sleeps. Her face goes blank as if she feels nothing for him. She knows that she is just pretending to be happy, to be all right, but inside, she is dead, cold, and empty. And Jake's presence can't bring her back to the Jena he knew. She opens Jake's wallet and takes out his credit card. At a corner store down the street, she buys hair dye and a pack of cigarettes. As the store clerk rings up the cigarettes, she speaks to Jena.

"You know smoking is bad for you, young lady."

Jena snatches the cigarettes from the clerk's hand and moves her face closer to the clerk's. "Yeah, well, so is hell," she replies. "You ever thought about that?"

The clerk stands back. Jena walks back to the hotel. There is a homeless man sitting in a corner near an alleyway. Jena stops and kneels down. She blows smoke in the homeless man's face. "Can I have one?" he asks.

Jena just stares at him. "I should kill you," she says. "Put you out of your misery. But looking at you, I can tell you're already dead. You're walking dead, just like me."

The homeless man is speechless. "Can I still have a cigarette?" he asks.

Jena stands up. "No. Just die quicker, and then you won't need to smoke or be homeless ever again." She walks away.

Upstairs, Jake is still asleep when she returns. Quietly opening the hotel room door, Jena is able to slip back into the room without Jake noticing. She puts Jake's credit card back in his wallet and goes straight to the bathroom where she spends hours getting ready for the club. *Tonight will be a new beginning for me,* she thinks. She stands in front of the mirror for hours staring at the red dress Jake bought her. She colors her hair red. With the red dress, red hair, the shoes, and the makeup Jena is wearing, she looks like a completely different person. She feels like a mature woman who just grew up from being a little girl. She stands in front of the mirror and makes poses like a woman who no longer thinks of herself as a child, but a person on a mission to make her life as meaningful as possible—even if it means killing someone else.

"Are you going to take all night?" Jake says, as he knocks on the bathroom door.

Jena doesn't reply. She stands without moving, without sound. The red hat sits on the side of the bathroom sink. She slides the hat over her head and slightly tilts it down so that it covers one side of her face. She opens the bathroom door and stands to the left of the door. Jake looks up from playing a game on his cell phone. He stands in complete shock at how beautiful Jena looks. The expression on his face tells her he is in total awe. He swallows. "You look ..." He can't speak for a moment. "Jena, you look so beautiful. You don't even look like you."

I'm not me, Jake, she thinks. "It is me, Jake," she says, trying to convince him. She walks toward Jake in a sexy and seductive way. "It's the new me." Jake wraps his arms around Jena's tiny waist. "Get dressed and ready so we can go."

Jake shakes his head. "Well then, let's go burn up the town," he says.

They catch a cab to the club. Outside the club is a line that wraps around the building. When Jena gets out of the cab, she looks like a celebrity. Everyone is staring at her. Too impatient to stand in a long line, Jena walks straight up to the door bouncer while Jake pays the cabdriver. The bouncer holds a guest list in his hand. "And who are you, miss?" the bouncer asks.

Jena looks the bouncer deeply in his eyes. "My name is Jena."

The bouncer stares at Jena's beautiful, red lips. "Jena Gray."

The bouncer is taken by her beauty and pulls the line divider back to let Jena enter the club. She looks back and points. Jake's running to catch up with her. "He's with me," she tells the bouncer. They both walk into the club like celebrities. Jena's confidence level is high. She no longer thinks of herself as Jena Parker, a shy young lady from a small town. She is now a high roller, an undiscovered, a member of the walking dead. Inside, the club is packed. People are practically breathing down each other's necks. The crowd ranges from young college students to middle-aged adults. When Jena walks into the room, all eyes are on her. Her beauty is stunning, and she knows that all the attention is on her—at least for tonight. Jake stands close to her.

"This place is crowded," he says. Jena stares around the room. "Hey, I have to go to the men's room." Jake taps Jena on the shoulder. She turns to him. Jake tries to yell over the music, "I have to go to the men's room!"

"I'll be at the bar," Jena replies. She walks to the bar and stands in the center with both arms bent back on the bar as she scans the dance floor. The music is blasting, and people are dancing everywhere. Jena leans on the bar and stares seductively at the dance floor. A middle-aged man and a young girl are dancing provocatively. They catch Jena's eye. *That man looks familiar,* she thinks to herself. The man dances closely with the young girl on the dance floor. He's wearing a tight polyester blue suit and a colorful shirt from the '70s. His hair is flopped over on one side. His belly flops over his pants, and he is completely drunk. Jena stares intently at the dance floor. Her face darkens. Her flush deepens with anger. Her eyes grow as black as a coal, and the hunger to kill sparks in her eyes like a lightning bolt when it strikes to kill anyone in its way. It was Mr. McNeil! *It's him! It's him!* she repeats over and over in her head.

CHAPTER TWENTY-NINE

Mr. McNeil had tried to change his looks slightly, but Jena knows who he is. She stands staring at the drunken Mr. McNeil and the young girl from the bar. Her expression grows angrier. Her face displays a horrible frown. She strolls to the dance floor. People are dancing, but just like a phantom, she moves smoothly through the crowd. Her parents' favorite song comes on, and the moment feels right. She pushes the young girl dancing with Mr. McNeil out of the way and starts dancing with him. She touches Mr. McNeil and herself all over as she dances. Mr. McNeil doesn't recognize her. He tries to move the hat, but Jena slowly moves his hands to her breasts and then up her dress. Mr. McNeil smiles. Coming on to Jena, Mr. McNeil tries to kiss her, but she pretends to push him away. She grabs his arm from behind her and dances him off the dance floor and out of the club.

Jake looks for Jena at the bar. He spots Jena leaving the dance floor with a man. He yells for her, but she doesn't hear him. Jena's total focus is on Mr. McNeil. She wants him dead in the way that a lover wants sex, in a way that a woman wants her dead husband back. The passion she feels for Mr. McNeil is far beyond the love Jake feels for her. It's far beyond the earth. Outside the club, Mr. McNeil waves for a cab. Jake is seconds too late to stop Jena from leaving. Just as he runs out of the club, the cab pulls off. "Damn it!" he says. He waves for a cab to follow them. Jena and Mr. McNeil's cab pulls up to a five-star hotel. With so much traffic, Jake's cabdriver falls a little behind. "Don't lose them, please." He panics. Sweat is dripping from his face. His cell phone rings. "Hello?" he answers.

"Jake!" His mother is on the other end. "Jake, honey, are you all right?"

"Yes, Mom, what's wrong?" he asks.

"How come you haven't been answering your phone or calling me back?"

"Mom, I'm in New York."

"New York? What are you doing in New York?"

"I found Jena, and well, she—"

Mrs. Paterson cuts him off. "You're with Jena? Jake, Jena mother's has been murdered. Kitty's dead." Mrs. Paterson starts to cry. "The police believe that Jena killed her, and she may also be involved in two other murders." Jake drops his cell phone. "Jake!" Mrs. Paterson calls. "Jake!" Her voice echoes from the cell phone on the cab floor.

"Drive faster!" Jake yells at the cabdriver.

Jena flirts with Mr. McNeil, and she touches his leg and moves her hands up his pants. Mr. McNeil kisses her chest and neck. She breathes out loudly. "I want you," he says. His very presence sickens Jena, but it isn't enough to stop her from getting revenge. Nothing and no one can stop her. In the hotel room elevator and hallway, Jena plays with McNeil. She gives him every impression that she is his for the night, that she wants him—and she does, dead.

Jena watches while a drunken Mr. McNeil searches for his room key. "Here, let me help you." She reaches in his pants pocket and finds the room key. He leans on the door and falls into the room as she opens it. She pushes Mr. McNeil on the bed. "Take off your clothes," she says in a sexy voice. Mr. McNeil removes his belt, pants, everything. He walks up to Jena to help her remove hers. "No, not yet," Jena whispers. Jena teases him.

He smiles and stumbles to the bathroom. "I have to go to the little boys' room," he says. "But when I get back, I want you naked in my bed," he says drunkenly. Jena begins to remove her dress. Mr. McNeil stumbles into the bathroom. Jena paces up and down the room quickly to try to find something to kill him with. She opens the hotel room drawer and finds a gun. She quickly takes off her clothes and stands naked in only her red high heels with the pistol held in her hands behind her back. Mr. McNeil stumbles out of the bathroom and tries to walk toward Jena but falls on the bed.

"That's good," she says. "I want you on the bed."

"Do you?" Mr. McNeil says while trying to sit up.

"Now, push your way up so I can see all of you clearly," Jena says.

"Come join me?" Mr. McNeil asks.

Jena pulls the gun from behind her back. "What are you doing?" he asks in a panicked voice.

"I'm not a little girl. I'm someone you know," Jena says. "Someone you took something from."

Mr. McNeil squints his eyes. "Jena?" He recognizes her. "Jena Parker? Is that you—"

Jena shoots Mr. McNeil once in the head. "No! My name is Jena Gray." Then she shoots him again in the face and twice in the chest.

Jake is in the hotel hallway and hears the gunfire. He opens the room door and tries to grab the gun away from Jena, but it's too late. "Jena, what have you done?"

Mr. McNeil's body lies dead and bleeding on the sheets. Jena stares at him. "Get out, Jake," she says.

"Jena, hurry up and get dressed!" Jake yells. He stares at Mr. McNeil. "We have to get out of here. The cops will be coming." Jake stares at Jena's naked body. His passion for her grows, and although Mr. McNeil is lying on the bed dead, all he can think about is making love to her. Jake hands Jena her dress. "Put it on; we have to go!" He tries not to stare at her naked body. Jena gently puts on her dress. Jake grabs her hand, and they rush out of the hotel room into a cab and head back to their hotel.

Both of them remain silent in the cab. Jake holds the gun in his hand. "No matter what you think, Jake, he deserved it. I'd kill him over and over again if I ever had the chance to. He murdered my father, and he murdered me."

Jake holds the gun and doesn't say a word. Finally, he asks, "Did he touch you, Jena?"

"You mean did he touch me? No."

Jake turns away and breathes a sigh of relief. The cab finally gets to the hotel room. Jena goes to the bathroom and stands in the doorway. "I'm going to take a bath." She slams the bathroom door.

Jake sits down on the bed and lays the gun on the table next to the bed. He begins to cry. He is torn between knowing the hideous things Jena has done and his obsession with her. He removes his shirt and sits on the bed. Jena walks out of the bathroom naked. She walks up to Jake. "Do you want me, Jake?" She lays him down on the bed and kisses him—first, gently on the lips and then down his chest to his pants.

She removes his belt; he turns her over. "Are you sure?" he asks.

"Take off your pants, Jake," Jena replies.

Jake removes his pants. He kisses Jena from her belly to her breast. His hot tongue gently licks her all over. Jena caresses his body and gives in to him. He stops for a moment. Hesitating and wanting her at the same time, breathing hard, he asks, "Jena, did you kill ..." Jake puts his head on her shoulder. Still breathing hard, he asks, "Did you kill your mother and those two other—"

Jena kisses Jake on the lips to stop him from finishing. She puts one finger over his lips. "Jake, please don't ruin this moment. Take me," she says. "I want you now, and you've wanted me forever."

He begins kissing and caressing her again. Jake's passion overtakes him. He doesn't care if Jena has just murdered a man or even if she murdered her mother. He stops and stares deeply into her eyes. "I love you, Jena," he says in a soft, passionate voice. "I love you so much." Jena doesn't say a word back. He continues to make love to her. She moans passionately. Jena begins to think back to the night she went to the library. Jake's body sways back and forth like a ship on the ocean.

His body movement takes her back, takes her back to the night she was raped. His body movement feels so familiar. *His cologne smells so familiar,* Jena thinks to herself.

"I love you, Jena," Jake whispers again.

She remains silent. *That smell,* she thinks. *That familiar smell,* Jena continues to think to herself as Jake makes love to her. *I remember that smell, these tender, but eager hands touching me. I remember.* Jena tries not to believe it could have been Jake. She flashes back to when they were playing as kids in the park and at school, to middle school when Jake always teased her, and to high school when he confessed his love to her. *That night at the library,* she thinks. *The librarian taps me on the shoulder and whispers that it's time to go. The red cup, Jake. It's all foggy. No. Jake was there. He met me at the door. "Drink this," he says. I remember now.* Jena thinks. *"It's really good," he says, so I drank it all. This moment, his body movement, and this familiar smell, I can't ... remember ... but wait. He held my hand and guided me to his room. I was dizzy, and then I felt my body fall to the bed. Were there three men? I don't know. Was it him? One face, two hands, his breath. What's wrong with me? It can't be Jake.* A voice speaks. *"It's him, Jena. He did it. Don't you remember his obsession with you? The constant drooling over you. Always hanging around trying to pretend he wanted to just be your friend, but all the while he only wanted one thing: all men want one thing, Jena. It's him!"* the voice yells.

Her body jerks. Tears run down Jena's cheeks as Jake continues to make love to her. After they make love, Jake kisses Jena gently on the lips. He pulls her next to him in the bed. He begins stroking her hair. "Jena," he whispers. "I've always loved you." Jena stares off into space. "I've always wanted you, but I didn't think you would ever want me this way. Making love to you is like making love to an angel."

Jena leans up in the bed. She reaches for the gun and points it at Jake. "Except, Jake, I'm not an angel," she says. "I know it was you. I remember now."

"Jena, no! Please, let me explain!" Jake yells.

Jena fires a shot. It hits Jake in the head. She watches while Jake dies. She sits up in the bed for a few minutes and then gets up to get dressed. She never looks back at Jake, but she doesn't have to; she knows he's dead. She can hear the blood drip from Jake's body onto the floor. Before leaving the room, she stops at the doorway. "Now you go. You go and tell somebody." She opens the hotel room door and closes it behind her. "Are you cold? Do you feel a chill running through your body? Well, I do. And I'll never be the same again."

THE END

CPSIA information can be obtained at www.ICGtesting.com
Printed in the USA
LVOW122354190112

264680LV00005B/8/P